The GLENELG COUNTRY SCHOOL

A *Margaret Wesley*
BIRTHDAY
BOOK

· presented in honor of ·

Priya N. Yadav

· given by ·

Mom, Dad and Pooja

see isabelle run

see isabelle run

elizabeth bloom

NEW YORK   BOSTON

Mysterious Press
Warner Books

Time Warner Book Group
1271 Avenue of the Americas, New York, NY 10020
Visit our Web site at www.twbookmark.com.

The Mysterious Press name and logo are registered trademarks of Warner Books.

Printed in the United States of America

First Printing: March 2005

10 9 8 7 6 5 4 3 2 1

Library of Congress Cataloging-in-Publication Data
Bloom, Elizabeth.
    See Isabelle run / Elizabeth Bloom.
        p.   cm.
    ISBN 0-89296-785-4
    1. Young women—Fiction.   2. New York (N.Y.)—Fiction.   3. Periodicals—
Publishing—Fiction.   I. Title.
    PS3569.A7882S44   2004
    813'.6—dc22

2004001949

Book design by RLF Design

Dedicated to the memory of
Sara Ann Freed
editor, mentor, and friend

With deepest thanks to:

Kristen Weber and Les Pockell
my valiant editors

Jimmy Vines
agent par excellence

Dr. James Terzian
for technical advice in forensic pathology

And most of all to:
David Bloom
for insights into the business world
(and for marrying me)

see isabelle run

isabelle leonard had never been good at job interviews. She never wore the right clothes, or said the right things,
or asked the right questions; she never charmed anyone, ever.
She'd sweat rings under the armpits of her silk blouse and, at
key moments, forget what was on her own résumé. As a friend
once put it: not only did she fail to put her best foot forward,
she actually wobbled on her high heels.

She'd always found it perplexing: Why did she come off as
relatively confident in the rest of her life, and as such a phe-
nomenal loser in the professional world? Why did she keep
screwing up so badly, even when she promised herself it would
be different this time? And more important, how exactly was
she going to pay her damn rent?

These and other questions were assaulting her brain as she
rode the elevator up to the forty-third floor of the Belden Building on a humid Tuesday morning. She tried to focus, but it was
no use. She knew she was going to make an idiot of herself.
Again.

Frankly, she considered it a miracle that she'd had the guts to get past the reception desk. One look at the Belden Building—a deceptively sedate name for a glass office tower that looked to stretch from the sidewalk to the ozone layer—had made her want to run the thirty blocks back to her apartment. But she couldn't, and not just because she'd already swapped her sneakers for heels. She needed the money. Desperately.

So she'd signed in at the front desk, gotten her visitor's badge, and stepped into the sleek silver elevator. She tried to psych herself up for the interview, the thought of which sparked both a churning in her stomach and a sour taste at the back of her throat. Suddenly fearful of halitosis, she grappled in her oversize purse for an Altoid, dumping half its contents onto the wing tips of a man in a thousand-dollar suit.

She tried to apologize. He walked out.

By the time she got to the forty-third floor, she'd managed to compose herself—sort of. She'd jammed everything back into the purse, chewed a mint, checked her lipstick and hair. The latter was falling out of the bun she'd fashioned with umpteen bobby pins, but it was too late to do anything about it. The elevator doors opened, and she was faced with another reception desk. She hesitated, took a deep breath, and stepped forward just as the doors were about to close on her pocketbook.

"Hello," she said. "My name is Isabelle Leonard. I have a ten o'clock appointment for a—"

"Well, *hello*," said the receptionist, a fellow brunette whose hair was in no way untidy. "It's just so *wonderful* to have you here. Everyone's just so *thrilled*." Her voice was a three-hundred-watt bulb, and Isabelle couldn't tell if she was (a) a sarcastic bitch or (b) a very friendly mental patient. "I hope you found us okay. Did you? And has anyone offered you some coffee? Would you like some? The coffee here's the *best*. I'd be happy to—"

"Er . . . no, thank you," Isabelle said, the lure of free coffee diminished by the prospect of dribbling it down her front. "I think I should probably just fill out my application."

"Oh, sure. Absolutely fine," she said, though she looked disappointed. "I'm just going to leave you in our Welcome Corner. You'll be snug as a bug." She handed Isabelle a clipboard and pointed her toward a small waiting area. When she came out from behind the desk, she proved to be wearing a flouncy floral skirt that matched her baby-pink sweater. "I'm just going to go get myself a little coffee," she said. "Just a little one. You sure you don't want any?"

"No, thanks. I'm fine."

"Super," the woman said. As she walked down the hall, Isabelle thought she was singing the title song from *The Sound of Music*.

Isabelle turned her attention to her application. *Name, address, Social Security number . . . Have you ever been convicted of a felony? Do you have any medical condition or disability which would prevent you from performing your duties?* Blah, blah, blah . . .

Filling in the blanks took her half an hour because she triple-checked her answers to make sure she hadn't misspelled anything. Then she sat there for another half hour until the receptionist returned, this time humming a tune Isabelle couldn't place.

"Oh, *no*," she said, eyes wide. "You're still here."

"I wasn't sure where I was supposed to go."

"Didn't I tell you?" Her well-plucked eyebrows came together. "I was sure I did . . ."

"I'm afraid not," Isabelle said.

"Oopsie. Well, it's the eighth door on your left."

Isabelle walked down the hall, counting doors until she got to number 8. The man behind the desk waved her in.

"You get all your paperwork filled out?" She handed it to him. "All rightie. You got any questions?" She hesitated, long enough for him to decide she didn't. "All rightie," he said again. Then he shuffled papers, asked to see her ID, and told her to go to office number 57-264.

She got back into the elevator and rode up fourteen floors, then navigated her way to the office. The desk outside it was empty—other than a phone, it didn't have so much as a stapler—and Isabelle wasn't sure what to do. She poked her head inside, but there was no one there. Finally, a man pushing a mail cart took pity on her.

"Hey," he said on his third pass, "are you waiting for Lisa?"

"I'm not sure. I'm here for a job interview in office number 57-264."

"Well, this is it." The man was in his mid-twenties, no more than five-five, with tousled brown hair and the compact build of a high school wrestler. He was dressed in business casual, a bright blue shirt tucked into khakis. Isabelle thought she saw the outline of a belly-button ring above his belt buckle. "Lisa's at lunch probably."

"I guess I'll wait."

"Might be a while. She's the queen of the three-hour lunch."

Isabelle bit her lip, then cursed herself for smearing her lipstick. "Oh."

"If you're gonna work here, you might as well read this." He pulled a magazine from a stack on the cart. The cover said *Becky* in big curly letters; beneath the name was a picture of the sexiest strawberry shortcake Isabelle had ever seen.

"Hey," said the guy, who was nothing if not perceptive. "You hungry?"

Hungry enough to kill you and eat you, she thought. But she just said, "Sort of."

"Wanna grab a sandwich?"

"Um, I don't think I should leave."

"You want me to bring you something?"

"I'm sorry . . . What's your name?"

"Trevor."

She stuck out her hand. "I'm Isabelle. And the truth is, if you got me something, I couldn't pay you back."

He examined her outfit. "Do my eyes betray me, or is that an Ann Taylor suit?"

"Former life," she said. "Right now I'm ready to eat my shoes."

"Okay," he said with a grin. "In the name of saving those lovely Ferragamos, I'll make you a deal. I buy you a sandwich, and you tell me how a girl in an eight-hundred-dollar outfit ends up dead broke."

"Thanks," she said, "but I'd just as soon starve."

. . .

She waited outside the office for two hours, by the end of which she was so hungry she would gladly have traded her entire personal history for a single chicken nugget. Finally, a fortysomething woman swept down the hall and into the office in a cloud of pricey perfume. Isabelle hung back for a few minutes, then knocked on the open door.

"Hello," she said. "My name is Isabelle Leonard. The personnel office said I was supposed to talk to you about a job."

"You're very late." The woman looked Isabelle up and down in a way that made her feel like she was being both scrutinized and ignored. Then she sighed, deep and aggrieved. "All right. Let's get started. What questions do you have?"

"Well . . . I guess I'm wondering what sort of work I'd be doing."

"They didn't tell you?" Isabelle shook her head. "Typical. You'll be my assistant, obviously. The job's been open way too long, thanks to personnel. You can touch-type, can't you?"

"Yes," she lied. "I can touch-type."

"Phone? Photocopy? Fax? All that?"

"Definitely."

"Good, because this is a very demanding department. They told you that, didn't they?"

"I'm afraid not. No one even said what department I was applying for."

Another head shake. "Special projects, of course. I'm the director. We plan very important events all around the world—not the everyday things that could run themselves, but events that are very important to Becky. *Personally.* I'll expect you as my right-hand person to put in as many hours as necessary."

"That's not a problem. I'm really eager to do whatever I can for the good of the company." Even before she'd finished the sentence, Isabelle knew it sounded rehearsed, which it was. "Honestly," she said, "I promise, if you hire me, I'll do a good job."

Lisa looked at her like she had a two-digit I.Q. "What do you mean if I hire you?"

"Well, I assumed you'd be the one making the decision, and—"

"Obviously, nobody told you anything," she said. "You've already got the job."

.   .   .

Isabelle spent the rest of the day setting up her computer and filling up her desk, getting lost as she wandered the hallways in search of supplies. She introduced herself to the people she met in her travels, but since she'd never had much luck with names, she wasn't confident she'd remember them. She also wasn't sure how long she was supposed to stay; by five-thirty, with Lisa already gone and the phone barely having rung, she couldn't think of a reason to stick around.

Isabelle flirted with the idea of a subway ride, but she couldn't bear to part with the cash. So she walked the mile and a half to her apartment on East 88th Street, the aroma of the hot-dog carts making her light-headed. She waved to the doorman on her way through the lobby, and he gave her his usual sympathetic look; the doorman knew exactly what was going on, because as a rule doormen know everything.

She lived in apartment 5-D—a one-bedroom that, unfortunately, looked like it belonged to someone who could afford an Ann Taylor suit. The rent was astronomical, but she couldn't find someone to sublet—and even if she ran away from the lease, she didn't have anywhere to go.

And the major reason for *that* was a jerk named Laurence.

Isabelle had met him back home in Vermont. He was on a ski vacation, she was temping at UVM and trying to figure out what to do with her life. He answered the question for her:

marry him, move to New York, change everything about herself. Being a lovesick fool, she agreed to all three. Then, precisely twenty-two minutes before the ceremony, he changed his mind.

Sweaty sneakers off, she sat on the edge of her futon and slathered peanut butter on Wonder bread, which had been on sale for eighty-nine cents at the bodega down the block. She washed it down with the one can of Diet Coke left in the fridge; she'd been saving it to celebrate when she got a real job.

"When I get my first paycheck," she told the can, "I'm buying more of you. And eventually, cable TV."

Not being able to afford cable television was, for Isabelle, its own circle of hell. Isabelle loved TV, from cop dramas to sitcoms to silly romances. Now all she had was whatever snowy images she could pull in on the rabbit ears. Sometimes, at night, she'd hear *Jeopardy!* or a *Law & Order* rerun coming from someone's apartment, and it was all she could do not to climb down the fire escape and watch through the window.

The prospect of being able to sign up for digital cable inspired her to drag herself over to her trusty Mac laptop, which was perched on a milk crate on the floor; her dad, who had been into ergonomics, would have been mortified.

He would have been equally mortified to know that the reason it was so situated was that she didn't own a desk—or, for that matter, much else in the way of furniture beyond the futon. For this, however, Isabelle had no one to blame but herself. All the furniture in the apartment had been bought to suit Laurence's taste; the day after he dumped her, she had called the Salvation Army and had it hauled away. The day after *that*, when she realized that she didn't even have a chair to sit in, she allowed that it hadn't been such a great idea.

So there she was, sitting on a pillow in front of a milk crate, trying to use her only skill to get herself out of financial purgatory. People had always told her she had talent, that she ought to write the Great American Novel. Now she just wanted to write something that'd pay for groceries. So far, her efforts hadn't been worth printing out.

She worked for half an hour on a novel she'd tentatively entitled *The Vampire's Deadly Kiss.* After reading the result out loud, she announced to the empty room that it stank, deleted it, and changed into the shortest skirt she had. Then she went downstairs and around the corner to a bar called Stella's.

She installed herself on a stool at the far end. It was turning into a bad habit.

By this time, the bartender knew better than to ask her if she wanted a drink—Isabelle never ordered for herself, because she was in no position to pay for an eight-dollar gin and tonic. She just sat there, knowing that if she looked waifish and lonely, some man would offer to buy her one.

The guy was buttoned-down and cocky as hell—as far as Isabelle was concerned, yet another Wall Street prick unwinding from a long day of breaking federal securities laws. He told her that no girl as pretty as her should be sitting at a bar all by her lonesome—he actually said it that way, verbatim—and before she'd seen the bottom of her first screwdriver, he was inviting her back to his place.

Isabelle made sure the man had a clear view down the front of her silk tank top as she leaned in toward him. Then she ran a finger along his dark-suited thigh and talked softly into his ear. "I'd love to," she said, "but there's one little problem."

The investment banker, or whoever he was, tilted his head

down so his mouth was a millimeter from her ear. "It's okay, gorgeous. Of course, you've got a boyfriend." He laid his palm against the curve of her waist. "I won't tell."

She pulled back, just slightly, and dropped her voice to a whisper. "That's not it."

"I don't see a wedding ring." He laughed, oozing confidence along with cologne. "Don't tell me you like girls." From the tone in his voice, Isabelle thought he'd like it very much if she told him exactly that.

"No," she said. "I like boys."

He was starting to get annoyed. "Then what is it?"

"The problem," she said, "is that I don't go to bed with assholes."

Back up in her apartment, after she'd changed into an old T-shirt that had belonged to her dad, she turned on the TV and fiddled with the rabbit ears. Then she crawled into bed and tried to watch an episode of *Friends*.

"My behavior," she told a snowy Lisa Kudrow, "is getting increasingly bizarre."

after eating another slice of bread with peanut butter for breakfast, Isabelle dressed for work in a pair of gray linen pants and a blue silk sweater set. For the millionth time, she thought that if the folks back home ever saw her like this, they'd bust a gut laughing.

Isabelle took a look at herself in the full-length mirror; nothing had changed in the past eight hours. Same flyaway brown hair, same tendency to slouch. A lot of guys thought she was too tall for them at five-eight; even those who didn't would agree that she was awfully light in the chest. People always said her green eyes were her best feature, but everyone knows that's the kiss of death. Tell some guy you want to set him up with a girl who has pretty eyes and a nice smile, and he assumes the rest of her is one hundred percent dog. At least she had a decent pair of legs, though she forgot to shave them at appropriate intervals.

Despite her degenerating mood, she decided to walk to the office; if she could keep it up, she'd get some exercise *and* save an extra twenty bucks a week for the TV fund.

When she got up to the fifty-seventh floor, she was glad to see she'd preceded her boss; being busy at her desk when Lisa came in would make a good impression. Unfortunately, though, Lisa didn't seem inclined to make an appearance.

Rather than dwell on the fact that her new job was shaping up to be a dud, Isabelle decided to check out back issues of *Becky*. She read each magazine cover-to-cover, going through issues devoted to holiday entertaining, gardening, weddings—she'd chucked that one to the bottom of the pile—window treatments, flower arranging, and the like. But there were also articles on more serious topics: recovering from eating disorders, leaving abusive mates, dealing with sibling rivalry.

Becky, Isabelle reflected, seemed to have parallel missions: she not only wanted to save the world, she also wanted to decorate it.

She was skimming through an article titled "Charming Slipcovers for the Battered Women's Shelter" when the phone finally rang; it was a jeweler saying that Lisa's bracelet was ready to be picked up. Isabelle gave her the message when she got in at ten-thirty.

"So don't tell me about it," she said. "Go pick it up."

By the time Isabelle got back, Lisa had already gone to lunch; Isabelle, who was catching on to the routine, figured she might as well go herself. She was sitting on a bench in the park across the street when Trevor sat down next to her.

"So," he said, "how do we like our new job?"

"I haven't really done anything."

"Well, you look good," he said. "Nice trousers. Don't tell me . . . Talbots?"

"You sure know a lot about women's clothing. Did you used to work in retail?"

"Nope. I'm just queer."

"Excuse me?"

"I'm a fairy. A ho-mo-*sex*-ual. Charter member of the boy-on-boy love club." He opened a white Pret A Manger bag and pulled out two sandwiches. "You want chicken or egg salad?"

"That's incredibly nice, but I can't eat your lunch."

"I got one for you. Saw you sitting there trying to choke down that hideous thing"—he indicated her uneaten P.B. on white—"and decided to stage an intervention."

"I, um . . ." She groped for a napkin. "Egg salad sounds good."

"Jeepers, Isabelle, are you crying?"

"It's . . . just been a long time since anybody did something nice for me, okay?" She occupied herself with unwrapping the sandwich. "So . . . what's up with Lisa? I mean, does she basically do nothing all day?"

Trevor shrugged. "Fits and starts."

"And how does she stay employed?"

"Old friend of Becky's. I guess she can do no wrong."

"Great."

"Hey, Becky Belden Multimedia's like any other big company. Some people work their asses off, other people get to skate."

"But that's not fair."

Trevor squinted at her. "Where do you *come* from, anyway?"

Isabelle ducked the question. "So how did the person who had the job before me deal with Lisa?"

"Marcia? I'm not sure. I didn't know her real well. She wasn't here very long." He'd suddenly decided to speak to his shoes, which were white leather with red designs; Isabelle wondered if he'd stolen them from a bowling alley.

"She get sick of counting paper clips all day?"

"Actually," he said, "she's dead."

"You mean like *deceased*?" He nodded. "What happened?"

"Crazy homeless guy pushed her in front of a subway. She was only maybe twenty-two. Seemed like a sweet kid, not a lot going on upstairs. She and Lisa made a hell of a pair."

"And what about Becky? What's she like?"

"Well, let's see." He pushed a stray lock of curly brown hair out of his eyes. "She's got her own TV talk show, plus the most profitable magazine *ever*, plus a load of products with her name on them, and she's richer than God . . . What would *you* be like?"

"Do you ever see her around the office?"

"Sometimes. Or else out at Shelby's Landing. That's her estate on Long Island."

"You've been there?"

"We get to go sometimes for, um, team-building events."

"Wow."

"Don't get too excited. It's really just an excuse to—"

"Pardon me," said a voice off to their left. They looked up and saw an elderly lady with a raincoat over her arm and an expectant look on her face. "I don't mean to bother you, but . . ."

Jesus Christ, thought Isabelle, *here we go again*.

chapter 3

"**aren't you that girl** from the *Post*?" the woman asked. "From the front page of the *Post*? You are, aren't you? I just want to say that I think you're awfully brave. And that dreadful man . . . I just wanted to spank him for what he did to you."

"Really, I'm sorry, but you've got me mixed up with somebody else."

"But you look so much like—"

"I, um, get that a lot," she said, concentrating on her sandwich until the woman finally gave up and went away. When she turned back to Trevor, his eyes were threatening to bulge out of his head.

"Oh my God," he said. "You're 'Give 'Em Hell, Isabelle.' I could kick myself for not putting two and two together. So come on, tell me all about—"

"No."

"Don't be such a clam," he said, swatting her on the shoulder. "You're a local celebrity, girlfriend. So tell Uncle Trevor—"

"I said no."

"Please? Pretty please with sugar on top? And a cherry?"

She gave him a look sufficiently venomous to shut him up. Then she fled back into the Belden Building, with a wounded Trevor announcing that he was going to Barnes & Noble to browse in the self-help section.

Give 'Em Hell, Isabelle. She could still see the two-inch-high letters blaring out from every newsstand in the city, as they had on a certain Monday morning not so long ago. She tried to get the image out of her head, but it seemed to want to stick there.

Luckily, as soon as she whirled through the revolving door, she was distracted by the crowd that was clogging one side of the glass-walled lobby, a dozen or so people jockeying for a view of something in a large display case. From what she'd seen of BBM so far, Isabelle figured it was either a perfect apple pie or a plea to help starving orphans.

"What an awful thing," she overheard someone say. "It's really such a terrible shame, don't you think?"

She was making her way to the elevator—and mentally chalking up one for the orphans—when she caught another snatch of conversation.

"You mean, he really just . . . disappeared? Like, poof? Can that really happen nowadays?"

Curious, Isabelle backtracked and elbowed her way through the crowd. The object of their pity was a glossy photograph of a young man in his early twenties, blown up to life size. He had scraggly brown hair and a dimpled chin; he was dressed in jeans and a T-shirt with a picture of a lobster on it. Sprouting from his left side was a profusion of oversize text. It took Isabelle a minute to realize that she was looking at an enlargement of an article from *Becky* magazine. The headline read, HAVE YOU SEEN OUR FRIEND?

The piece told the story of one Kenny Chesbro, a pale-looking fellow who worked in tech services. Apparently, Kenny enjoyed playing vintage video games and collecting *Six Million Dollar Man* memorabilia. He had an adoring family, a pet ferret, and a mountain bike he liked to ride in Central Park on the weekends.

And six weeks earlier he'd vanished without a trace.

The story, set to run in the upcoming issue of the magazine, was BBM's attempt to spread the word about his disappearance. According to the police, he was last seen leaving his apartment in Brooklyn. His parents were offering a twenty-five-thousand-dollar reward for information leading to his safe return, but so far, there had been no solid leads.

"Sounds like a nice guy," Isabelle heard a woman say.

"Yeah," said another. "Betcha he killed himself."

.   .   .

When she got back to her desk, Lisa was waiting for her. From her demeanor, Isabelle thought her lunch must have consisted entirely of double espressos.

"Where have you *been?*" she said. "I've been looking for you for *hours.*" Isabelle opened her mouth to answer, but Lisa waved her off with a sputter of spastic hands. "Whatever. I can't be worried about the time. There's too much to do. I want you to set aside everything else you're working on. I have a project for you."

"What kind of project?"

"A *special* project, of course."

"Oh . . . Okay." She grabbed a pen and notebook. "What would you like me to do?"

"I've had the most remarkable idea." Her grin was so wide Isabelle was beginning to shift her diagnosis from caffeine to Wellbutrin. "Becky's going to love it. So what we need to do is put together a *very* thorough proposal. I'm going to handle the overall planning, of course, but I'll need you to do lots of research."

"What sort of project is it?"

She clapped her hands, *rat-tat-tat*. "An executive retreat, timed for the week after the IPO. And not just upper management but midlevel, too. About fifteen hundred people."

"I'm sorry but . . . what's an IPO?"

Lisa gave her an exasperated look. "An initial public offering of stock. BBM is going public in February. On *Valentine's Day*. Becky's going to make individual heart-shaped quiches for the entire stock exchange. The whole company's been talking about it for months. How could you possibly not have heard?"

"Sorry, I just started. So you need me to find someplace in the city where we can hold the retreat?"

"In the city? Oh, no. That isn't the way Becky does things. Look for places in the Caribbean, or perhaps the South Pacific. The Mediterranean is lovely, too. Find out where we could hold it, what sorts of amenities they offer, transportation, everything. I'd like to have at least a dozen options to choose from. And the proposals have to look first-rate. I'm not just going to send them to Becky—we'll need copies for all the V.P.'s and an even more detailed workup for Bill Friedrich."

"Um . . . who's he?"

Another exasperated look. "The director of corporate communications, of course."

Isabelle wrote it down. "And what's the budget for the trip?"

Lisa stared at her, her expression even more disapproving. "I'm sure we can worry about that later. Don't let's limit our options. Like Becky says, 'Bighearted people don't think small.'"

"And when do you need it by?"

"Day after tomorrow."

Isabelle tried to push down the panic. "But aren't you out of the office for that"—Isabelle grappled for the term— "personal enrichment seminar?"

"So I am. Tomorrow, then."

Tomorrow? Her panic took a giant leap. "But, um . . . since this is my first project for you, I want to do really well. I'd hate to rush it and mess up."

Lisa looked skeptical, but she didn't argue the point. "Well, all right. But make sure you have it ready for me first thing Wednesday when I get back." Isabelle promised she would and spent the rest of the afternoon checking out resort Web sites and playing phone tag with the company's corporate travel agency.

She tried not to let the photos on the Web sites get her down, but she couldn't help it. There were too many happy couples gazing at each other across candlelit dinner tables, or walking hand in hand through the surf. Goddammit, she was supposed to be one of them. If things had gone as planned, she'd have gone to a tropical island a couple of months ago; she'd probably still have her honeymoon tan. But instead, she looked pasty and depressed—which accurately reflected how she felt.

Three hours later, when Isabelle was still trying to come up with even *one* place that satisfied the fifteen criteria Lisa had laid out, she got the distinct feeling that someone was spying on her.

It wasn't a tingle-at-the-back-of-the-neck sort of thing; she just could've sworn she heard some heavy steps outside her cubicle, but every time she looked up there was no one there. She finally got up, peeked around one side of the partition—and ran into a sixtyish woman carrying a stack of papers. The woman shrieked and dropped the papers, which scattered on the floor; she tried to gather them up, but since she looked to weigh nearly two hundred pounds, she had a hard time bending over. Isabelle did it for her.

"Oh, thanks, hon," the woman said. Her accent was as heavy as she was; not being from New York, Isabelle couldn't tell if it was Brooklyn or the Bronx. "You're an angel."

"Have you been waiting to talk to me?"

"Me? Oh, well . . . I was wondering, since you're new here and all . . . do you fax?"

"What?"

"The fax machine. Do you know how to run it?"

"Sure, I guess."

"Woo-hoo. So could you help me out?" Isabelle didn't respond; she was powerfully distracted by the woman's dress, a tentlike affair covered in purple and lime-green flowers. "So could you?"

"Okay." She followed the woman down the hall. "What's the problem?"

"It keeps hanging up at the end of every page. Drives me bananas."

"Did you just start here, too?"

"Nah, I've been here three years. I'm just no good with the fax."

It took Isabelle thirty seconds to diagnose the problem, which was that the woman wasn't feeding the sheets in fast enough. She showed her how to put the whole stack in and let the machine feed them automatically; the woman clapped her hands and asked Isabelle if she wanted a cup of coffee.

"Thanks, but I should probably get back to work."

"What, you never heard of a coffee break?"

"Sure, I . . . Okay."

Isabelle followed as the woman lumbered down the hall; she usually wasn't an uncharitable person, but it struck her that her new friend waddled like a gigantic duck. Eventually, they reached a door marked BECKY BELDEN FAMILY LOUNGE, which turned out to be filled with wooden tables and overstuffed couches. Most were already occupied; after getting coffee from a silver-plated urn, the two of them found a spot in the far corner.

"Wow," Isabelle said. "This is really nice." She looked over at the cart, topped with a platter of muffins and pastries. "Is today some special occasion?"

"What?" The woman waved a doughy paw dismissively, then bit into a cheese Danish. "Nah. It's always like this. Becky knows how to treat her people. You met her yet? No? Well, wait till you go out to Shelby's Landing for team-building. Place is so ritzy it makes you wanna pee your pants."

Isabelle took a bite of her cinnamon roll. "Team-building?"

"That's where you get to experience the true specialness of the BBM family," the woman said, clearly regurgitating the contents of some motivational pamphlet. Then she leaned forward, snowing crumbs onto Isabelle's lap. "Where are my manners? I haven't even introduced myself. I'm Loretta. From subscriber services."

"I'm Isabelle. Special projects."

Loretta extended a sticky paw, and Isabelle shook it. Without meaning to, she found herself ogling the woman's plate, which was so full it was impossible to see the china under all the carbs. When Loretta noticed her gaze, she waved in the direction of the plate and leaned even farther forward.

"I don't usually eat this much," she said in a half-whisper. "It's just, right now I'm a teensy bit upset. Did you hear the awful news?"

"You mean, about Kenny . . . somebody? The one who disappeared?"

Loretta frowned at her. "Who? No, I mean about *Doreen*. Doreen *Fusco* from circulation. She passed on yesterday."

"Oh. I'm sorry."

Loretta made a clucking sound and started nibbling on a rugelach. "So sad. Gal my age gets run over on Northern Boulevard. That place is a *death trap*. You ever go there, honey, you gotta look both ways before you cross. Promise me?" Isabelle nodded. "Good. Now, would you be an angel and get me one of those yummy crescent rolls?"

It took Isabelle half an hour to make a polite exit. It wasn't until days later, when she was curled up on her futon with one of the old issues of *Becky* she'd pinched from storage, that she gave the woman another thought.

The piece was headlined HEARTBREAK OF A MAFIA MOM, with a long story about a lady who'd lost her home after her husband was shot in the head and her three sons went to jail on racketeering charges. But it wasn't the article itself that got Isabelle's attention; it was the photograph.

The woman in the picture was her new friend, Loretta.

chapter 4

it would never have happened if she hadn't had that first drink. She'd always been a lightweight; she should've known better than to let Trevor buy her a martini. A *green-apple* martini. What was it, anyway? All she knew was that it tasted like a lollipop dissolved in NyQuil, and it went straight to her head.

It'd all started when Trevor ambushed her outside the main entrance, called her a closet case, and told her he was taking her "somewhere fabulous." It proved to be a bar in Chelsea with lots of low velvet couches surrounding glass coffee tables. Five of Trevor's friends were there, young men in tight polyester shirts and even tighter trousers, and from the greeting she got when she sat down, she could tell one thing for sure.

He'd told them.

At that point, she definitely needed a drink. Trevor ordered for her, which is how she ended up with the liquid lollipop. She took a slug, felt the alcohol burn down her throat, and turned to Trevor. "You," she said, "are a little bastard."

"Come on, you can't blame the boys for wanting to meet you." The young men smiled en masse. One of them leaned in and put a hand on her knee. "I just want you to know how amazing I think you are," he said. The others nodded, like they'd choreographed it.

"Lucky me." She drained her drink.

"So tell us everything," said the fellow on the far left.

Isabelle made an agonized strangling sound and leaned back. She narrowed her eyes, and the five men on the banquette turned into ten. "Fine," she said, still sober enough to realize how drunk she was. "It's like this. Once upon a time, a girl met Prince Charming. He asked her to marry him, and she spent all the money she could scrape together on a fancy wedding. And then . . . he didn't show up."

Trevor shook his head and patted her hand. "The *bastard*."

"He stood her up at the altar, and he cashed in her plane ticket and went on the honeymoon to Fiji with her best friend, where by all reports they had a fine time drinking cocktails out of coconuts. And the girl"—Isabelle rubbed her face; it appeared she was losing muscular coordination as well—"made an ass of herself."

"You did *not*," said one of the guys. "You went to the reception and danced on the tables and had a ball. I saw the pictures."

"*Every*body saw the pictures," said another.

Trevor made a smooching sound an inch from her hair. "You kicked butt, missy," he said. "You gave all New Yorkers an object lesson in the importance of not being defeated by circumstances."

Isabelle opened one eye. "Read that editorial, too, did you?"

"Don't make fun," he said. "Instead of curling up and playing dead, you told everybody at the church to come party on down. That took guts."

"If you say so."

"Seriously, Izzy," Trevor said, handing her a second drink that seemed to have appeared from nowhere. "Think how cool that is. You go stag to your own wedding reception, and the photographer shoots a picture of you shaking your booty in your big white dress and you end up on the cover of all the tabloids. What a rush."

"'Give 'Em Hell, Isabelle,' said one of the indistinguishable five. "What a headline."

"Oh, yeah," she said, "I'd *much* rather have that than a husband."

. . .

Isabelle's hangover was something spectacular; when she woke up the next morning, she saw blinding dots of light that seemed to bore straight into her brain. She was desperately thirsty and her teeth hurt; she dragged herself into the shower and tried to remember how many of those awful martinis she'd put away the night before. She got to five and stopped counting.

She was twenty minutes late to work, but there was no one around to notice—Lisa being at a spa in the Berkshires for her "personal enrichment seminar." Isabelle sat at her desk, downed two more aspirin, and decided that if she looked at any more resort Web sites, her head was going to explode.

Her headache was just starting to abate around eleven when she heard a crowd approaching from down the hall. There were about a dozen of them—half BBM employees, the rest Japanese businessmen in dark suits.

"We're here to see Ms. Kinne," one of the employees said.

"Er . . . your name, please?"

The man looked annoyed that she didn't know him by sight. "I'm Jeffrey Bing, vice president for human resources. These are our guests from the Nakatomi Group. Could you tell her we're here?"

"I'm afraid she's not in."

He scowled at her, like it was her fault. "There must be some mistake. We had an appointment. There was a memo."

Another BBM type stepped forward. This one was much taller and less hostile. "Can you check her schedule? Maybe she's coming back soon."

"I'm afraid she's out of town." Isabelle wrestled with the computer's scheduling program. "Um . . . it doesn't look like she had the appointment written in for today." She pushed a few more keys and found an entry that said, JAPANESE PUBLISHERS—SITE VISIT. "Oh, here it is. I guess she put it in for next week."

"What's your name?"

Isabelle gulped. She told him.

"I'm Bill Friedrich from corporate communications," he said, as though he were greeting a new member at the country club. "Please tell Ms. Kinne we're sorry we missed her." He smiled at her as he spoke. His companion, on the other hand, gave her a look that said, *Please tell Ms. Kinne she's in big trouble.* Then everybody kept going down the hall.

Isabelle sighed and shook her head. She hoped that if Lisa ever got fired, she didn't get sacked along with her. She was still thinking about it when a girl in a miniskirt, boots, and black-framed glasses showed up at her desk. "Hey," she said, "are you booked this afternoon?"

"Um, yeah. I have a ton of work to do."

"Know anybody else who can use a ticket? We really need warm bodies. Tour group from Kansas City had to cancel."

She held out a rectangle of stiff pink paper that said, THE BECKY BELDEN SHOW, JUNE 27, 3:00 P.M. Isabelle snatched it. "Er . . . maybe I can make it."

At the appointed hour, Isabelle went outside and reentered the building through another door, capped by a small marquee with the show's title. She handed her ticket to a guard and was directed to a special elevator that took her and a clutch of eager middle-aged ladies to the fifth floor. A look around the studio convinced Isabelle that there were two kinds of people in the audience: ecstatic tourists and employee conscripts. It was easy to tell them apart: the former tended to be a lot larger, happier, and less fashionable. A few were wearing homemade T-shirts that said, WE LOVE BECKY, with a heart replacing the word "love."

As the hands on the studio clock moved past three, the sounds of shifting bodies and chitchat got louder. Then the houselights dimmed, the stage lights went up, and a man in his thirties came out carrying a microphone. He thanked everyone for coming and reminded them that, for Becky, people like them were all that really mattered. When he got to the end of his spiel the lighting shifted and he asked the audience to join him in welcoming their host. Within seconds, the studio had erupted into a clapping chant. *Becky! Becky! Becky!*

Then the music swelled, and out walked Becky Belden.

chapter 5

She's shorter *than I expected her to be,* Isabelle thought, then felt stupid for thinking it. It was such a stereotype, and Isabelle hated to think of herself as so unoriginal. But there was no arguing that Becky Belden was short, as legends go. She couldn't be much more than five-two—and it had never occurred to Isabelle that she might actually be taller than Becky.

The woman may not have much in the way of height, Isabelle thought, but she had plenty of charm. There was something self-effacing about her, something appealingly homey. She'd been like that on the phone when she told Isabelle how brave she was and said she should come in and ask about a job. And although she'd wanted to run a story about her in the magazine—Becky said her readers would consider her an inspiration to young women—she didn't even mind when Isabelle said she'd rather not.

"All that matters is helping you get back on your feet." That's what she'd said, and Isabelle had been grateful for it.

Becky was dressed in black crepe slacks and an ice-blue silk blouse. She wore a single strand of pearls around her neck and a black headband in her blonde hair. Her makeup was understated; she wasn't even wearing earrings. Becky's whole demeanor said that even though she was the star, she wasn't the most important person there; no, what really mattered were the guests and the audience.

Today's guests were all women, and though they didn't seem to have much in common, it turned out that they'd been victims of the same incompetent, drug-addicted ob-gyn. Some of them had chronic pain, some were sexually dysfunctional, some were sterile; they'd sued for malpractice and gotten a big settlement. But, as one of the guests put it, "money can't give me back my womanhood."

As if the story weren't sad enough, Becky and her heartfelt questions somehow managed to make it seem even more tragic. Then, after the second commercial break, she brought out a surprise guest: the doctor himself. Up until then, Isabelle had managed to keep from crying. But the guy was such a mess—so sorry and self-flagellating and *broken*—that she completely lost it.

After the show, still red-faced and sniffling, she returned to her desk and put in another few hours on the executive-retreat project before deciding to pack it in. Feeling tired and oddly beaten up, she laced up her sneakers for the walk home. She wondered whether she could afford to splurge on take-out Chinese for dinner—a question that occupied her brain so fully she didn't notice the man standing over her.

Eventually, she did.

"Um . . . can I help you?"

"I'm looking for Lisa Kinne. This is her office, isn't it?"

"Yes, it is. I'm afraid she's out of town."

"Is she expected in next Thursday?"

"Hey, wait a minute. Aren't you the guy from *The Becky Show*? The one who warms up the audience?"

Isabelle thought the skin around his hairline turned a bit red. "Sometimes."

"I saw the show today. You were really good. Are you an actor or something? You kind of look like one . . ."

"Not exactly."

"Oh. Are you, like, a professional emcee? Because you did a really good job at getting the crowd all—"

"I'm an executive vice president." She stared at him, wondering if she'd managed to get herself fired on her third day at work. Then he smiled, which made her decide not to fling herself down the elevator shaft. "One of Becky's idiosyncrasies. She decided I was the man for the job, so I do it. No use in pushing back on the boss when she's got her mind made up."

"Oh, I . . . Listen, I didn't mean to sound—"

"Don't worry about it."

"Um, about that message you wanted to leave for Becky—" She tripped over her tongue. "I mean *Lisa* . . ."

His smile turned into a smirk. As far as Isabelle was concerned, it didn't make him any less attractive. "I'd like to schedule a meeting with her."

"Regarding?"

"We're considering a project, and we want her feedback."

"Um . . . okay. I'll give her the message."

"Thank you." He glanced at her nameplate. "Isabelle Leonard. What kind of name is that?"

"My dad was Jewish. My mom was French."

"I see. So you'll give her the message?"

"Sure."

He thanked her and took off down the hall. It wasn't until Isabelle was ten blocks from home that she realized she'd forgotten to ask his name.

.   .   .

When she got to work the next morning, it was waiting on her desk.

Maxwell Collins. That was all, just the two words on a yellow sticky note. The handwriting was precise, each letter exactly the same height, perfectly centered on the paper square. Who was he, anyway? She went to the Becky Belden Multimedia Web site and found a link called "The Becky Belden Family." She clicked on "senior management," and there he was—a short bio and a head shot with a clenched-teeth smile.

> *Maxwell A. Collins has been part of the Becky Belden Family for seven years. He is an executive in charge of BBM's internal consulting section, responsible for helping the company run at peak efficiency. He holds an undergraduate degree from Duke University and an MBA from Harvard. Mac, as his friends call him, lives in Manhattan. In his spare time he enjoys sailing and competing in triathlons.*

She was still staring at his photo when the phone rang. "Lisa Kinne's office."

"Isabelle Leonard, please."

She recognized the voice. She looked back at the screen and smoothed her hair, as though he could see her through the pixels. "Um . . . this is Isabelle."

"This is Mac Collins. Turns out I don't need that meeting with Lisa, so if you've scheduled it, you can cancel."

"Do you want me to leave her a message?"

"Not necessary. I'll be in touch if I need anything else," he said, and hung up.

Seeking to avoid looking at more resort Web sites, she started to organize her desk, which she'd already turned into a mess of pens and Post-it notes. She was on her knees, going after an errant bottle of Wite-Out at the back of the bottom drawer, when she noticed a piece of paper stuck along one side.

It turned out to be a photograph of a young couple Rollerblading. They were both on the nerdy side, clad in helmets and kneepads, and though they seemed in danger of breaking their necks, Isabelle thought they looked awfully happy.

She turned the photo over. On the back was handwritten *Marcia & Jim, Central Park, 4th of July*. Isabelle slipped it into the top drawer, figuring she'd try to return it. Then she remembered something Trevor had told her, and pulled it out again.

The photo had to belong to the previous occupant of her cubicle. Which meant that the young girl smiling on Rollerblades was no longer breathing.

. . .

Ignoring Trevor's entreaties to go out for a drink, Isabelle spent Friday night at home eating frozen pizza and listening to her snowy TV. When her alarm went off before dawn the next morning, it was all she could do to drag herself out of bed and go to her other job. For the past month, Isabelle had been waitressing at a diner in Midtown, a family-owned place that barely did any business on the weekends.

But it had been the only thing she could find; no other restaurant would hire her without any experience, not in this economy. The Greek owners—who, like most of the eight million residents of New York City, felt sorry for her—offered her the breakfast-and-lunch shift on Saturdays and Sundays. It meant she had to get there at five-thirty, fill up ketchup bottles and cream pitchers, and bring plates of pancakes to whoever wandered in.

The diner was called the Cosmopolitan, and today the name seemed more ridiculous than usual. There were almost no customers, and those who did show up tended to look one step up from street people. They didn't tip well. So far, her biggest windfall had come from a studious-looking blond guy about her age, who'd left a ten-dollar bill on a six-fifty order.

But at least she liked her employers, Greeks who'd emigrated thirty years ago but sounded like they'd just come off the boat. Mr. Mendes, balding and paunchy, fit right into his surroundings, but his wife didn't look like someone who owned a diner. She was whip-thin, her hair was dyed jet black, and she wore coral-pink lipstick at six o'clock in the morning. So far, she'd tried to set Isabelle up with her son, two cousins, and a nephew who didn't speak English.

Isabelle was filling salt shakers and staring at the clock, counting the minutes until she could go home and wallow in self-pity, when Mrs. Mendes told her she had another customer.

"Hi," she said to her order pad. "Can I get you some coffee?"

"Coffee would be great."

"Regular or . . . *You?*"

Maxwell Collins was sitting there grinning at her, wearing an old blue T-shirt and a pair of jeans. Isabelle looked down at her uniform, a polyester number in a shade of yellowish pink that made her look like she had jaundice, and contemplated the fact that she wanted to die.

isabelle's initial instinct was to run into the kitchen and hide behind the deep fryer. Upon later reflection, she wasn't sure that standing there with her mouth half open was much of an improvement.

"What are you doing here?"

"Having brunch."

"You? Here? Are you serious?"

He peered toward the end of the counter, where Mrs. Mendes was pretending to read her Greek newspaper. "Your boss know you talk to the customers like that?"

Isabelle redirected her attention to her order pad. "So . . . what can I get you?"

"What do you recommend?"

"Tuna melt."

"Then a tuna melt it is."

"Are you serious?"

"That's twice you've asked me that inside thirty seconds.

And my answer is yes"—he peered at her name tag—"yes, *Isabelle*, I am entirely serious."

"Oh, for Pete's sake, you know my name." She chuckled despite herself. "Now, do you ser—" She cut herself off. "Do you *actually* want a tuna melt?"

"As a matter of fact, I'm a big fan of the tuna melt. And I'm still interested in coffee. If you're not too busy."

She looked around the near-empty diner. "I think I can manage it."

"Thanks."

"You want fries?"

"Naturally."

Isabelle clipped the order slip to the metal carousel and spun it around to face the kitchen. She was retrieving the coffeepot when Mrs. Mendes grabbed her by the elbow and dragged her into the corner.

"Cute, yes?" She was trying to whisper, but it came out loud enough to be heard on the sidewalk.

"Huh?"

"The new customer," she rasped. "He's good-looking man."

"He's someone from my office."

"He work for Becky, too?" Mrs. Mendes was a rabid fan.

"Yeah. I guess he's a pretty big deal."

"Wowie." Mrs. Mendes' eyes widened. "Handsome *and* rich." She started futzing with Isabelle's hair, which was falling out of its ponytail. "You go put on makeup. I serve the coffee."

Mrs. Mendes reached for the pot, but Isabelle yanked it away. "I don't have any makeup."

The older woman's neon lips formed a disapproving purse. "What you mean you don't have no—"

"I mean I don't have any *here*." She looked over her shoulder at Collins, who was doing the *Times* crossword. "Now, can I please get him some coffee?"

Mrs. Mendes' expression segued to a pout, but she stopped grabbing for the pot. Isabelle picked up a cup and saucer and went back to Collins' booth.

"Um . . . sorry that took so long."

"You know an eight-letter word for 'shell dweller'? Starts with 't'?"

She thought about it. "Terrapin?"

"Fits," he said, and wrote it down.

"Your tuna melt'll be up in a minute."

"I'm not in a hurry. I'm taking the day off even if BBM falls down around my ears."

"It's Saturday, anyway."

He set the puzzle aside. "*You're* working."

"I don't have a choice."

"Aren't we paying you enough?"

"Not nearly."

He grinned and took a sip of his coffee. "What about the warm and fuzzy feeling you get from working for Becky Belden? Doesn't that make it all worthwhile?"

She shrugged. "It doesn't exactly pay the rent."

"Where do you live?"

"On the Upper East Side."

"I'm down in Chelsea."

"Oh." Her eyes widened. "*Oh.*"

"Jesus, don't look at me like that. Not every guy in Chelsea is gay."

The bell rang, and Isabelle was on her way to pick up the

order when she saw Mrs. Mendes had beaten her to it. Then she realized that the woman was carrying *two* tuna melts.

"Here you go," Mrs. Mendes said, putting one on Collins' aqua place mat. Then she waved the other in front of Isabelle's nose. "Time for your lunch break. I figure you two keep each other company, yes?"

"Uh, thanks, but I really should be"—Isabelle tried desperately to think of something—"filling up the ketchup bottles."

"Well, I clearly can't compete with that." Collins' expression was neutral, but Isabelle thought he was laughing at her behind those blank blue eyes.

"Ketchup?" Mrs. Mendes said, the tuna melt still in midair. "Who needs to worry about ketchup? We got plenty." She put the second plate down with a whack and slid the Heinz bottle between them. "Now sit," she said, and walked off.

Isabelle turned back to Collins, face aflame. "Sorry."

He finally cracked the hint of a smile. "Oh, for chrissake, just sit down and don't worry about it."

She sat, but once she was settled into the vinyl booth, she couldn't look him in the eye. She stared down at her food, the orange cheese melted over towering mounds of tuna salad.

"Aren't you hungry?"

She looked up at him. "I'm *always* hungry."

"Really?" He sounded impressed.

"Yeah. I pretty much eat like a pig every chance I get."

What was she saying? She always did jabber like a fool when she was nervous.

"And you like french fries and tuna melts?" She nodded. Nodding seemed safe. "You know, you're not like any other woman I've ever met. Where do you come from?"

"Vermont."

"Where? I've been skiing up there—Killington, Stratton . . ."

"Farther north, almost to Canada. We call it the Northeast Kingdom."

"That's romantic."

The word made her blush. What the hell was wrong with her? Was she really so starved for affection that she was reduced to idiocy by a pair of blue eyes and a tuna melt?

"So," he said, "how did you end up in the city?"

"Long story."

"I've got time."

"Long, *boring* story."

"Why don't you let me be the judge of that?"

She opened her mouth and closed it again. Then she said, "I moved here to get married. The guy stood me up at the altar, stuck me with a lease I can't afford, and then went and had a fling with my maid of honor. So here I am." She blinked. "Oh my God. I cannot *believe* I just said that."

"Is it true?" She nodded. "Then you're mistaken. That story is neither long *nor* boring."

"I guess not," she said, then collapsed into a fit of chuckles. "I guess it sure as hell isn't."

"And when did this happen?"

"A few months ago."

He gave her a look. "Wait a second. You aren't—"

"*That* Isabelle. I'm afraid so." She felt at ease all of a sudden, though she had no idea why. She leaned back, put her feet up on the empty side of Collins' seat, and took a bite of her tuna melt; it was cooling but still tasty. "So what's *your* story? I told you mine, you tell me yours."

"I grew up in Connecticut. My dad worked on Wall Street. I went to Duke, worked on Wall Street for a while, got my MBA, worked as a consultant for a couple of years, then came to BBM."

"And you're really into your job?"

She thought she saw something unpleasant flit across his face. "I used to be. Right now I'd say my job is really into me. Today's the first day I haven't gone into the office in . . . hell, I don't even know how long. Months."

"So what are you going to do?"

He looked surprised. "I haven't thought about it."

"There's a million things to do in the city, right? Especially if you've got money to spend."

"I take it you're on a pretty tight budget."

"That's an understatement."

He flashed her a smile. "Didn't you at least hock the engagement ring?"

"Family heirloom. His mother asked for it back right there at the church."

"Ouch. Okay . . . If *you* had a day off in New York, and you could do anything you wanted, what would it be? Come on, sky's the limit. Broadway show? Dinner at some hot new restaurant?"

"I . . . Forget it. You'll just laugh."

"I will not. I swear."

"I always wanted to take that boat cruise—you know, the one that goes all the way around Manhattan?"

"You mean the Circle Line?" She nodded. "Out of anything you could do in the city, all the art and culture, you want to go on the Circle Line?"

"You promised you wouldn't laugh."

"I know," he said, "but I didn't think it'd be the Circle Line."

"Well, that's what I'd do, okay? First I'd go to Chinatown and eat as many pork buns as I could, then I'd go on the sunset cruise around Manhattan, and if I had any money left over, I'd go to a movie. One with lots of car chases."

He looked at her for so long she was starting to feel like a bug under a microscope. Then he slapped his palm on the table. "Let's do it. The pork buns and the movie and the goddamn Circle Line."

"But . . ."

"But what?"

"I can't afford it."

"Don't worry. They pay me a lot. What time do you get off work?"

"No problem," Mrs. Mendes yelled from across the room. "She just finish her shift." She turned to Isabelle with an exaggerated wink. "*Right?*"

chapter 7

when it was over, and she was back in her apartment, she sat on the bed and tried to figure out if she'd just been on a date.

Yes, he'd paid for everything, but he'd known up front she didn't have any money. Yes, he'd opened doors for her, and he'd let her wear his sweatshirt on the boat, but that was just good manners. Wasn't it?

He hadn't tried to hold her hand at the movies; that awkward moment when they'd both reached for the Junior Mints at the same time was just a fluke. And he hadn't tried to kiss her good night. As a matter of fact, he'd slapped her on the shoulder. There was nothing even remotely romantic about it.

So why had she gone all goony in Chinatown? She thought it had started when he held out a pork bun he'd bought in a crowded, closet-sized shop and told her to take a bite; after all, feeding someone is a pretty intimate act. Or maybe when he told her to stand still, and he tipped her chin up and wiped something off her cheek. She'd tried not to look into his eyes, but she'd flunked. And at that moment, she could've sworn he was going to kiss her. When he didn't, it was something of a letdown.

You're a spoiled brat, she said to herself. *You get to spend the day doing exactly what you want, for free, and now all you can do is pout about the kiss you didn't get.*

So was it a date? She couldn't decide, and she couldn't think of anyone she could talk to about it. She sure wasn't going to confide in Trevor; that would be equivalent to putting it on the employee Listserv. She thought about trying one of her friends back in Burlington, but she didn't pick up the phone. Even if any of them still wanted to talk to her, the idea of calling to babble about some guy just a matter of months— weeks, really—since her aborted wedding was humiliating.

There goes Isabelle again, getting all wound up about some fancy guy she can't have. Not for long, anyway.

She tried to read a three-week-old *Time* she'd lifted from her neighbor's recycling bin, but she couldn't concentrate. She turned off the light and lay there, trying to convince herself that the city noise was what was keeping her awake.

.   .   .

She might as well own up to it: she'd spent her entire Sunday shift at the Cosmo hoping Mac Collins would show up. Never mind that he'd said he was going to work all day. She'd been hoping he'd drop in; she'd even hidden an English muffin in a corner of the kitchen in case he wanted a tuna melt.

But he didn't show—and to make matters worse, even her customers seemed to notice she was acting like a lovesick fool. The big tipper from the previous day had come back, but although he'd distinctly asked for pancakes, she'd put in an order for French toast.

"You seem distracted," he said. "Is there something wrong?"

The man was blond and slender, and he had nice eyes; if Isabelle hadn't been so distracted by memories of Mac, she might've thought he was cute.

"It's nothing," she said, hoping a friendly smile might restore her tip. "I'll go switch these right away."

"Thank you. I don't much like French toast."

"Here, let me warm up your decaf."

"It's tea," he said, just as she was sloshing coffee into his cup.

The day went on like that, with Isabelle keeping one eye on her customers and the other on the front door. At home, she found the light on her answering machine maddeningly steady: no message from Mac. When she got to work the next morning, she held her breath as she logged on to her computer, but there was no e-mail from him, either.

Luckily, she didn't have time to brood about it. She needed to finish her research for Lisa by Wednesday morning, and she was nowhere near done; she worked straight through lunch without realizing it.

"Hey, hon," said a woman's voice. "How about you and me go for a little teeny-weeny coffee break?"

She looked up, and there was the lady from down the hall, the one she'd had coffee with before. She couldn't remember her name, but she remembered the headline: HEARTBREAK OF A MAFIA MOM.

Isabelle was about to refuse when she realized she was starving. One of those cinnamon bear claws, with which she'd been supplementing her food budget for the past week, sounded pretty good.

She followed the woman down the hall, hoping she'd

remember her name before it got embarrassing. They went into the break room, and Isabelle filled her china cup with Guatemalan Antigua, topping a glass plate with a bear claw and two miniature corn muffins.

Loretta, she thought as they sat down. *Phew.*

"So," the woman said through a raspberry Danish, "you married? Got any kids?"

"No."

"Smart girl. Kids are nothing but heartache. I have three sons, and they're in jail. All three. Not together even. Separate."

She tried to feign surprise. "That's awful."

Loretta shook her head and went *tsk-tsk-tsk.* "They were good boys, too. Didn't always do right things, but they were always good to their mama. And now I gotta work for a living. Can you imagine?" She shrugged her hefty shoulders. "Thank God for Becky."

"Becky?"

"She heard what happened, and one day out of the blue she called me up and offered me a job. Didn't matter that I didn't have experience or nothing. She just said, come on in. And I'm not the only one, neither. There's lots of people around here owe Becky like I do. She's a real special lady."

. . .

As usual, Isabelle's coworkers started filing out at the stroke of five, as though they were responding to a dog whistle she couldn't hear. They changed into their commuting shoes and packed their paperback thrillers for the train, some wearing MetroCards around their necks. By six-thirty, the whole department had cleared out, leaving her alone in the office for the first time.

But Isabelle wasn't entirely by herself; she had her humiliation to keep her company. She'd been feeling it ever since she'd had coffee with Loretta and found out that she was just one of a passel of strays that Becky had picked up. It was bad enough to be a charity case—but to be in the same league with a woman who couldn't even run the fax machine was pathetic.

She tried not to think about it, to concentrate on the mountain of research she had to do, but she couldn't. Her writing teachers had always told her to channel her feelings into her work, so she booted up the word-processing program and read over her latest stab at mass-market fiction. Since the vampires hadn't been working out, Isabelle had shifted to Westerns. She tried to imagine her words in print, with her name on the cover. As it was, though, she had a hard time picturing her prose printed on a roll of toilet paper.

She sighed and went back to work, only to sigh again and wander down the hall in search of coffee. There was no one else on the floor—workaholics like Mac were headquartered elsewhere—and the atmosphere struck Isabelle as oddly downcast. Most of the denizens of Becky Belden Multimedia were so relentlessly upbeat that during working hours the office had an aura that Isabelle had taken to calling creepy-chipper. Now, with the flouncy furniture and inspirational slogans visible only in the half-light of a few fluorescent bulbs, it had the desolate air of a packed-up circus.

Forget creepy-chipper; working alone at night for the first time, Isabelle thought the office was simply creepy.

chapter 8

Despite the vaguely unsettling atmosphere, Isabelle was in no hurry to leave. She had nothing to do at home but stare at the blizzard that passed for her TV set. And, if she was going to admit the truth, she was worried that if she left the office, she'd wind up in another upscale bar—trying to cheer herself up by attracting, then rejecting, some buttoned-down investment banker.

She siphoned a cup of coffee from the silver urn in the break room, but it must've been sitting there for hours; she took a sip, found it tepid and chalky, and spat it into a wastebasket. The pastries had been cleared away, so she didn't even have the option of a stale croissant for dinner. Feeling herself slide into a pout, she went back to her desk and tried to organize the stacks of information she'd collected for Lisa, but she couldn't concentrate. She leaned back in her chair and gave her self-pity an all-access pass.

Once upon a time, she'd had a life. In high school, she'd been fairly popular. And in college, she'd been downright cool, at least among the crunchy intellectual set. But at twenty-four, she was a failure. She had no man, no kids, no career; she didn't even have a coffee table. The closest thing she had to a friend was Trevor, whom she barely knew. Her parents were dead, and her only relative was her sister, who lived on the other side of the country and with whom Isabelle had nothing in common. Sure, she'd recently gone out with a good-looking MBA. But what were the odds that he wasn't going to turn out to be another six-figure jerk?

No, all she had was this stupid job, playing handmaiden to Lisa's ego. Why anyone with half an ounce of talent would want to work here was beyond her. The last girl who'd had her job must've been brain-dead.

The thought brought her up short. The last girl who had her job, she realized, *was* dead.

That fact made her laundry list of misery sound like the whining that it was. Feeling ashamed of herself, Isabelle opened her top drawer and fished out the photo she'd found the week before.

Marcia & Jim, Central Park, 4th of July.

There they were, wobbling on Rollerblades, looking as happy as Isabelle had ever seen two people look. If the photo had been taken last summer, Isabelle knew exactly where she herself had been: in the Hamptons with Laurence and his ad-agency friends.

Neither couple, she reflected, had lived happily ever after. But at least *she* had lived; that was something to be grateful for.

Isabelle stared at the photo, running a fingernail along Marcia Landon's round face. She felt bad about keeping it, but her attempts to locate "Jim" had failed. In fact, no one at BBM had any idea that Marcia even had a boyfriend. Isabelle had asked Lisa if there was a relative she could send the photo to, but Marcia didn't have any family. With a put-upon tone in her voice, Lisa had informed her that she herself had packed up Marcia's things, now languishing in a storage room on the twenty-third floor.

Compelled by a burning desire to procrastinate, Isabelle headed for the elevator. Maybe she could find an address book or something that might help her track down the elusive Jim.

The elevator doors opened on twenty-three, to near pitch-blackness. Isabelle stepped out automatically, but as soon as the doors closed behind her, she regretted getting off. She eyed the Up button, but decided to keep going; nothing bad could happen to her down here, no matter how dark it was. Could it?

She felt her imagination start to go postal, and she reined it in with a laugh. Considering how easy it was for her to picture herself getting offed by some maniac—call him the Skyscraper Slasher—it was a wonder she wasn't a better fiction writer.

She made her way down the hall, searching for the lost and found; Lisa had said that Marcia's things were in a storage room across the hall from it. It was still dark—the only light came from a crack in a door somewhere up ahead—but her eyes had adjusted so she could read the nameplates on the rooms and offices. The light got stronger as she went, the sliver becoming a slice and then a swath across the rose-colored carpet.

It hadn't occurred to Isabelle that the storage room might be locked. Well, it was too late to worry about it. She kept going until she got to the brightly lit stretch of carpet. On one side of the hall was the lost and found; it was hard to miss, since the door bore a needlepoint square with the following message:

Lost your hat?
Dropped your glove?
We'll return them both . . .
. . . with love!

Isabelle swore under her breath. "Who the hell *are* these people?"

The door across the hall was ajar, light spilling out and making her blink. Obviously, the storage room wasn't locked. But was there someone in there?

She listened outside the door. Hearing nothing, she went inside and started looking around for Marcia's stuff. The room was filled with white cardboard boxes, some labeled with people's names, others with notations like TECH SERV XMAS DECORATIONS—DO NOT PILFER!

Isabelle toured the room for a box bearing Marcia's name, finding it high up on a shelf in the corner. She dragged a stepladder over and pulled it down, then hauled it across the room to where the light was better. Camped out on the carpet, she opened the box and encountered a riot of desktop tchotchkes. There were Smurfs and Beanie Babies and funny-shaped pencils, scented erasers and Gumby dolls and a troll with pink hair. She counted three framed photographs, all of the same cat, and a half dozen figurines from a science-fiction movie Isabelle couldn't place. She pulled out a Magic 8 Ball, asked it if she was ever going to have sex again, and disliked the answer.

She was an odd duck, that one, Loretta had said. Isabelle wouldn't argue with her.

Digging further, Isabelle found what she'd been hoping for—an address book—though she hadn't anticipated it would come covered in fuchsia faux fur. She was opening it when she heard voices coming down the hall.

Isabelle froze, surrounded by Marcia Landon's adolescent menagerie. What should she do? Rifling through someone else's property wasn't exactly kosher. Still, she was only doing a good deed; she wasn't doing anything that could get her fired. Right?

The voices got louder, coming close enough for Isabelle to realize that they belonged to two men. There was no way she could get out of the storage room unseen. Should she just stand up and greet them? Her other choice was to hide behind a stack of boxes like a sniveling coward and hope that they didn't see her.

Again pondering the likelihood of getting canned, she jammed the tchotchkes into the box with all deliberate speed.

Then she dove behind the boxes and hoped for the best.

chapter 9

The Two men came in a second later.

"You sure we have to get all of them tonight?"

"You know we do. Why ask?"

A martyred groan. "It'll take at least one more trip."

"It'll take what it takes. Has to be done."

"It's the Chesbro thing, don't you think?" the first man asked. "It's got everybody freaked out."

From her perch behind the boxes, all Isabelle could see was their shoes and pant legs. They looked expensive, so she obviously wasn't hiding from a couple of janitors—which made her glad she'd taken the coward's way out.

"It's the Chesbro thing for sure," the first man continued. "It's too big a wild card. Could bite us on the ass."

"It already has," said the second. He was wearing what Isabelle recognized as Bruno Magli wing tips, a staple of Laurence's wardrobe. It didn't make her like him. "And frankly, I've had it with playing defense. It's about time we pushed back on that little creep."

"You said it."

"Going forward, we'd better make sure this kind of mess doesn't happen again. Because I for one am sick to death of cleaning it up."

Isabelle heard the thud of something being loaded onto something else. Then came a squeaking sound, the rubbing of wheels against carpet.

"How many more after this?" asked the first man in a tone that said he already knew.

"Seven."

"Jesus."

They wheeled their cargo down the hall, and Isabelle decided it was an excellent time to get out of there. She slipped the address book inside the waistband of her slacks, a tactic she'd seen in countless police dramas, and carried the box over to where she'd found it.

But the shelf was empty. A few minutes ago it'd been filled with other boxes; now they were gone. The shelf beneath it still had some boxes—Isabelle counted seven—but the one underneath that one had been cleaned out, too.

What should she do? Putting the box back would be like advertising that someone had swiped it. Should she take it with her? Isabelle dismissed the idea. What if she ran into them in the hall?

She decided to stick the box behind one of the others in the still-full row, in the hope that they'd assume they'd missed it. But why in the world were two guys in expensive shoes clearing out boxes in the middle of the night?

The boxes that were left all seemed to have names on them, so Isabelle figured they were individual property. Some were yellowed, like they'd been there a while. Curiosity prompted her to pull one off the shelf, but she instantly decided that lingering was stupid; she had no idea how soon the two men would come back. After peeking out into the hall to make sure the coast was clear, she sprinted for the fire stairs. She hiked up five flights, then took the elevator back to her office. She tried to sit at her desk, but there was too much adrenaline whipping through her body.

She stuffed the address book into her purse, took the express elevator to the lobby, and walked home. All thirty blocks, she kept asking herself the same questions.

What were those two guys up to?

What, if anything, did it have to do with poor, dead Marcia Landon?

Was she crazy, or did the one in the fancy wing tips sound a little like Mac Collins?

And hadn't she seen him wearing the exact same shoes?

·   ·   ·

Isabelle had never killed anyone, though she'd wanted to. If she could've gotten away with strangling her ex-fiancé, for instance, she was fairly sure she would've done it.

Now the throat she longed to throttle belonged to Lisa. Why? Come Wednesday afternoon, Isabelle had knocked on her door and asked what she thought of the options for the executive retreat. Here's what Lisa said:

"Oh, are you still working on that silly thing? I decided that's not such a good idea, after all. I could've sworn I said something . . ."

Isabelle was on the point of telling her that she goddamn well had *not*, when she remembered that her job was the main thing between having a roof over her head and living out of a grocery cart in Riverside Park. So she clamped down on her tongue, went back to her desk, and tried not to scream.

. . .

That night, Isabelle gave in to Trevor's pleading that she come to his place for a "tiny little get-together." Isabelle hadn't been to Trevor's apartment, but once she found it, she wasn't sure how she'd get home in one piece. He lived in a fifth-floor walk-up in a part of the East Village called Alphabet City, which struck Isabelle as a folksy name for someplace where the *cops* are probably afraid of getting mugged.

Trevor's apartment turned out to be a studio so small the bathroom sink was in the living room. There was no kitchen, just a hot plate and a microwave.

"Oh, wow," Isabelle said. "Is that a Murphy bed?"

"You come in here, and *that's* the thing you notice?"

Isabelle looked around the room and realized that it was filled with dozens of mannequins in various states of undress. Some were posed in funky tableaux, while others were stacked like corpses. They took up at least a third of Trevor's living space.

"What *is* all this, anyway?"

"It's what I wanted to show you. It's my *passion*."

"Please don't tell me you want to be a window dresser."

He struck a pose that echoed the nearest mannequin. "It is indeed my dream to practice the art of the vitrine."

"Can I have that drink now?"

He mixed her up something he called a vermouth cassis; it was sweet, and it went down smooth. Probably too smooth.

"Hey," she said once they'd been enveloped by Trevor's furry beanbag chairs, "why are you so dressed up?"

He fiddled with his thin black tie. "Memorial service."

"Oh my God, I'm sorry. I didn't know a friend of yours died."

"Wasn't a friend exactly, just someone at BBM I knew from doing deliveries. Died of meningitis a few weeks ago." Isabelle's eyes widened, but he waved her off. "Don't worry, it wasn't the infectious kind. Happened pretty fast—one day he felt fine, a couple days later he was dead."

She was quiet for a minute, then took a liberal slug of her purple drink. "Is it just me," she said, "or are people at this company dropping dead left and right?"

chapter 10

Trevor eyed her over his glass. *"Pardonnez-moi?"*

"Think about it. There's that girl Marcia, who had my job before me. She got pushed in front of a subway train by some homeless nut. And then there was this lady I heard about in circulation who got run over by a car in Queens. Plus, on my first day on the job, there was a sympathy card going around for some guy who worked in P.R. who died of an allergic reaction or something. And now there's your friend."

"So that's . . . what? Four?"

"Doesn't that sound like a lot?"

Trevor shrugged from his prone position. "In a company of three thousand people who live in *this* city? Not really."

"But those are just the ones I heard about, and I don't know *any*body."

"Actually," he said, "if you count Pinkie, it's five."

"Pinkie? Who's Pinkie?"

"Chick who worked in the mail room with me. Real wastoid. OD'd a couple of months ago."

"Okay," she said, "so there's five. And plus there's that guy who disappeared, Kenny somebody from tech services. What do you think is up with that?"

"I have no idea."

"Trevor, the guy *vanished*. Don't you think he's probably dead, too?"

"What's your point? You think somebody's stalking us? Or maybe we're cursed? Like BBM was built over an Indian burial ground?"

"Hardy-har-har."

"Hey, come on, lighten up," he said. "Please tell me you're not seriously freaked out."

"No, but . . ." Isabelle debated whether to tell him what she'd been up to; when she looked back on it later, she figured the liquor had tipped the scales toward revelation. "If I tell you something, do you *really* promise not to say anything to anybody?"

"I'll be the soul of discretion."

"I mean it this time. If you blab, you could get me fired."

"Cross my heart and hope to die." He waggled his eyebrows at her. "No pun intended."

Isabelle told him about her late-night adventure. When she was done, Trevor didn't even try to restrain himself from snickering.

"That's it? A couple of guys move some boxes, and you think there's a conspiracy?"

"I didn't say that. I don't know what is going on. But moving those boxes and talking about that missing guy—don't you think it's weird?"

"Izzy, this is Becky Belden Multimedia—an international corporation based on the ego of one rich lady who knows eight hundred ways to fold a napkin. Of course, it's weird."

"Well, what do *you* think they were up to in the middle of the night?"

"Who cares?" He reached for the crème de cassis bottle. "Did you at least find a way to track down Marcia's guy?"

Isabelle nodded. "There was a Jim in her address book, all doodled up with hearts. He still hasn't e-mailed me back, though."

Trevor stirred his drink and licked the spoon. "Then mission accomplished."

"Hey, don't you think what those guys were doing was a little odd?"

"I think you watch far too many one-hour crime dramas."

"Thanks a lot." Isabelle looked at her watch. It was almost eight. "Hey, when's everybody else coming over?"

"It's just us."

"But I thought you said you were having a get-together."

"We are," he said. "You, me"—he waved toward the mannequins—"and my friends."

.   .   .

Even as a child, Isabelle had known that things are never like you picture them. When her parents took her to Disney World, after years of begging on her part, the whole place had seemed *less* than she'd imagined. Nobody really lived in Cinderella's castle, and the "It's a Small World" ride was just a bunch of dolls.

Even New York, which Isabelle had dreamed of via the pages of John Cheever and Damon Runyon, didn't seem particularly special once she got a good look at it. It was a place where people lived, like any other—except there were an awful *lot* of people, and they always seemed to be vying for the same six inches of sidewalk.

So it was with some astonishment that she got her first look at Shelby's Landing. She'd seen Becky Belden's estate on the North Fork of Long Island in photographs and TV shows, but when she got there, she had to admit they didn't do it justice. The place was like something out of a storybook, with its gabled main house overlooking the bay, and the clutch of barns and little cottages dotting the landscape. There were flowers everywhere, riots of them, and friendly animals who seemed content in their immaculate pens.

The whole place had an unreal air, Isabelle decided. It reminded her of something she'd seen outside Paris on a trip with Laurence—the miniature farm Marie Antoinette had built at Versailles so she could pretend to be a simple milkmaid while the crowd outside the gates yelled for her head.

But if Shelby's Landing seemed like a stage set, Isabelle couldn't deny that it was beautiful. It was; even the imposing security gate, which featured a painting of the golden retriever the estate had been named after, had a genteel quality. Inside the twelve-foot fence, there were greenhouses growing every kind of flower and vegetable you could think of. If Becky Belden wanted to make an omelet, she could use eggs from her henhouse and cheese made with milk from her herd of goats. Anchored off her private dock was a sailboat, named *Good Manners.* Isabelle hadn't gotten a look inside the garage, but it was big enough to hold an entire fleet of cars.

Becky Belden knew how to live.

Isabelle had gotten to Shelby's Landing around ten o'clock that morning, one of a yawning vanload of BBM employees who'd left the city at quarter of eight. They were welcomed by Becky herself, casually dressed in jeans and a white fisherman's sweater. She said she hoped they'd enjoyed the muffins she'd baked for their trip, and invited them to come into what she called the rumpus room.

This turned out to be a space the size of a small movie theater, furnished with puffy couches and lots of pillows. Becky went up to the front, accompanied by a cadre of female assistants, and the next thing Isabelle knew, they were singing an inspirational song about the importance of hospitality, the lyrics projected on a screen at the front. Then Becky said good-bye, explaining that she had to get to the city for that afternoon's TV taping. Once she was gone, one of the assistants took the mike and said it was "sharing time."

"This important exercise is all about letting the people you work with get to see the real you," the woman said. "Every day, we go to the office, and we only bring a tiny bit of ourselves through the door. So we want you to open up, to share the things in your life that are truly important. Of course, you don't have to say anything you're not comfortable with. But Becky wants everyone who works with her to know that his or her fellow employees are three-dimensional human beings . . ."

A woman to Isabelle's right gave a little sigh, like she was thoroughly touched. What was wrong with these people?

"You'll notice that there's a video camera in the back," the facilitator was saying. "That's so your important, individual thoughts and feelings can become part of BEA." She pronounced it *be*, as in the verb. "That's Becky's Empowerment Archive. It allows anyone in the company to learn a little something about anyone else—all you have to do is go to the Friend-ship Center on the thirty-first floor and look at the person's recording. It's just another one of the many ways in which Becky has worked so hard to make BBM a special place where people's individuality is so highly valued . . ."

The woman kept talking, but Isabelle stopped listening. She was busy worrying that she might actually have to participate in this idiotic exercise—or, even worse, that she might have to go first.

Luckily, when the leader asked for volunteers, the woman at Isabelle's right started waving her hand. She was chosen, bounded off the couch, and sat in an upholstered chair up front. There, eyes aglow, she answered questions about her hobbies, family, tastes, et cetera. Isabelle thought it sounded like she was taping a personals ad.

Eventually, it was her turn. She couldn't avoid it, unless she wanted to make a spectacle of herself by declining—which she'd been told would be "absolutely okeydokey" but which no one else had done.

She walked up to the front. It felt like she was going to the gas chamber.

chapter 11

"**What's your name?**"

"Isabelle Leonard."

"Where did you grow up, Isabelle?"

"Vermont."

"And what brought you to New York?"

She opened her mouth to tell the truth, then remembered that she wasn't under oath.

"It seemed like an interesting place to live."

"What's your job at BBM?"

"I'm an administrative assistant in the special projects department."

"Where do you live?"

"Manhattan."

"Are you married? Do you have children?"

"Um . . . no. I mean, neither."

"Relax, dear," the woman said. "Pretend you're talking to someone nice you just met at a cocktail party. Now, what about your parents? Where do they live?"

"They're both deceased."

"Siblings?"

Again she resisted the impulse to tell the truth. "No."

"Is there a special someone in your life?"

"Er . . . not at the moment."

"Isabelle, what's your favorite thing to do when you're not at work?"

"I like to read."

"And what do you like to read?"

"Books."

The woman was starting to look frustrated. Clearly, Isabelle wasn't shaping up to be the teacher's pet.

"If you could have three wishes," she asked, "what would they be?"

"Um . . ." She could feel herself starting to sweat. "Cable television. I don't have it right now."

"And what else?"

"I'm not sure."

"Oh, come on," the leader said. "There must be *something*."

"I . . . I'm not sure."

The woman's eyes narrowed. Isabelle got the feeling that she couldn't wait to get her out of the chair so she could move on to a more cooperative victim.

"Well, then, how about if you share something with us that no one else knows about you?"

"Uh . . . what kind of thing do you mean?"

"Oh, just anything. What's something you like to do, or a favorite food—something that people who know you at the office wouldn't necessarily expect?"

"Oh." Isabelle grappled for something profound. "Well, I like to take baths."

"How nice. Tell us more."

"You know, long baths with candles and oils. And listening to the radio."

"Go on."

"I've got this boom box I've had since high school. Sometimes I listen to mix tapes."

"Yes? And what else?"

"Sometimes I read in there. It's, um, relaxing."

"That's lovely, just lovely," she said. "Now, does anyone here have a question for our new friend, Isabelle?"

To Isabelle's great relief, no one did.

.   .   .

He showed up again on Saturday.

Isabelle had no idea what to make of it. Not a word for an entire week, and then there he was—sitting in a booth, reading the *Times*, and eating a tuna melt. Or, more specifically, *two* tuna melts.

"That one's for you," he said, pointing at the cheese-covered mounds.

"Really? When you ordered it, I thought you were just a glutton."

"Sit down."

"I've got other customers, you know."

"The place is deserted. I bet Mrs. Mendes can handle it."

"What are you doing here, anyway?"

"I'm madly in love."

She gulped. "You are?"

"With the tuna melts. They're really fantastic. So why don't you eat yours before it gets cold?"

"Very funny," she said. But she sat down; the tuna melt did

look good. And so, if she was going to be honest with herself, did Mac Collins. He was wearing jeans again and a faded T-shirt that said, HARVARD: THE DUKE OF THE NORTH.

Had he been one of the men in the storage room? Isabelle had given the question a fair amount of thought, but she still didn't have an answer. She was pretty sure she'd seen him wearing the same kind of wing tips, but that could just be a coincidence. She thought she'd heard Mac use some of the same turns of phrase as the mystery man, but she wasn't certain about the voice. And even if it had been him, Trevor was probably right. The more she thought about the whole episode, the sillier it seemed.

"So," he said, "what's on the schedule for today?"

"I don't have any plans."

"I meant, what are *we* doing? Surely, you've got another perfect New York day percolating in that head of yours."

"But—"

"Didn't you have fun last time?"

"Of course I did. But—"

"You said you don't have any plans. So come on. If you could do anything in the city, what would it be? Other than what we did last week, of course."

"Are you serious?"

"Don't tell me we're going down *that* route again."

Isabelle opened her mouth, then realized she didn't know whether she wanted to yell at him or just laugh. Finally, she said, "Coney Island."

"Really?"

"I've never been there. I've always wanted to ride the Cyclone and have one of those Nathan's hot dogs. And I like to play those carnival games where you shoot at the ducky and never win. And now they have this minor-league baseball team—"

"You like roller coasters and minor-league baseball?"

"Is that weird?"

"Yeah," he said, "but in a good way."

. . .

On roller coasters, Isabelle had always been a screamer. She loved to go over big drops, straight down so your stomach flew up into your throat, and yell her lungs out. When they got off the Cyclone, Mac looked dazed.

"Was that the ride," she asked, "or was that me?"

He bought her three hot dogs and watched while she ate them; he said his stomach hadn't recovered. He told her he'd get something at the ballpark—but when they tried to go to the Cyclones game, it was sold out. Mac didn't seem perturbed; he just walked a few yards from the main gate and gave a scalper an obscene amount of cash for a pair of tickets. The game was terrific—a regular home-run derby—and on their way out, he insisted on buying each of them an official Cyclones cap. They wore them on the subway, and Isabelle thought they sure *looked* like a couple.

"So," she said as he walked her to her building, "am I right in assuming that I won't hear from you all week, and then you'll turn up at the Cosmo on Saturday?"

"Does that sound so bad?"

"It's a little weird."

"It's all I can do right now." He sounded serious all of a sudden. "Would you rather I didn't show?"

"No, I . . . It's okay. It's probably all *I* can do right now, too."

"Then I'll see you next Saturday," he said, and gave her another swat on the shoulder. This time, though, she was absolutely sure she would've preferred a good-night kiss.

. . .

The call came in at a karmically inopportune time. Just as Isabelle was sitting at her desk cursing Lisa for being a clueless, unappreciative word-that-rhymes-with-rich, the phone rang.

"Good, you're there. Fantastic. I need you to come over right now and help me with something. Okay? I'll see you in fifteen minutes."

"Um, Lisa? I'm sorry, I don't . . . You need me to come where?"

"To my apartment, of course. I'm *telecommuting.*"

Lisa made the word sound important, like she'd coined it herself.

"Well, okay. What do you need me to do?"

"It's something I'm working on. It's a surprise. So definitely don't tell anyone. Now, before you leave, I need you to go down to supply and get me some more glue sticks. And see if there's any more poster board. If there's not, I'll have to send you out later. And look for some glitter—the kind that comes in tubes. That'd be just *super.* Okay? Get here as fast as you—"

"I'm afraid I don't know where you live."

"What? Oh." She gave the address, which turned out to be only a few blocks from Isabelle's own. "Now get over here ASAP, all right? And since you're probably going right past there, you might as well pick up my dry cleaning on your way. Okay? Great!"

isabelle got to Lisa's apartment in forty-five minutes, and only because she'd taken a cab—for which she dearly hoped she'd get reimbursed. From the other side of the door, she could hear the piercing bark of what she feared was going to be the kind of yippy beast her dad had always called a rat dog. When Lisa opened up, she had a half-wild expression in her eyes and a scrap of paper stuck to her cheek.

"Ooh, good, you're here. Come on in and sit down and I'll tell you everything. Did you get my dry cleaning? Great. Don't mind Sprinkles. He won't hurt you. He's a perfect little princess." She turned to the dog, a tiny Yorkie with a pink bow in his hair. "You're my pretty-pretty princess, aren't you, sweet pea?"

Trying to keep a straight face, Isabelle maneuvered past the dog and took a look around the apartment, which was decorated with much better taste than she'd anticipated. There was a big, comfy couch and an oak coffee table; the only bit of wretched excess was a canopied dog bed that looked to have been stolen from the palace of Louis XV. But the thing that grabbed her attention was the flat-screen TV complete with DVD player and TiVo digital video recorder—the stuff of Isabelle's fondest audiovisual fantasies.

"Okay, okay," Lisa was saying. "Sit down right there on the couch. Are you ready? Are you excited?" Isabelle tried to pry her attention away from the TV. The dog jumped up on the couch and perched in her lap. "All right. Just wait there. I'll be right back."

Lisa went into another room and came back with a giant piece of poster board, which she unveiled with a flourish.

"The Best of Becky," she said, gesturing toward the paper like a spokesmodel on *The Price Is Right.* "It's a coffee-table book. A compilation of all the best articles from the magazine, to commemorate its tenth anniversary. That's just a few months after the IPO, so *imagine* all the publicity we'll get. Look, I did a mock-up of the cover." She ran her hand along the edge of the bright pink rectangle. "It's got a big picture of Becky right here in the middle and copies of the nicest magazine covers all around the edge. What do you think? Don't you love it? Isn't it the best idea *ever?*"

It actually was a pretty good idea. Isabelle was amazed that Lisa had come up with it.

"So here's what we're going to do," Lisa was saying. "You and I are going to go through all these back issues of *Becky*"— she gestured at the stacks next to the couch—"and we're going to pick the best ones. I've been working on it for hours, but it's too much for one person. And don't be scared—I'll help you. You don't have to make any decisions by yourself."

Isabelle was halfway to telling her that she was confident a magna cum laude double major in philosophy and English literature would give her a solid footing to clip articles out of old magazines, but she kept her mouth shut. It wasn't just because she wanted to keep her job; she also didn't have the heart to rain on Lisa's parade. The woman was obviously having the time of her life. And considering that she had a huge oil painting of Sprinkles hanging over the couch, Isabelle didn't suspect Lisa had much of a life to begin with.

Her boss ordered in for lunch, which they ate on the floor surrounded by glue sticks and magazine scraps. Isabelle was surprised when Lisa proffered a bottle of Alsatian Riesling, which she said went well with Chinese food. Isabelle took a glass just to be polite, but the idea of mixing white wine and kung pao chicken struck her as revolting. Lisa didn't seem to share her distaste; she drank most of the bottle herself and opened another.

The wine made her talkative. Isabelle heard about Lisa's early life as the only child of older parents, about the succession of small dogs that she enumerated like Tudor kings. She waxed nostalgic about playing the flute in her high school marching band and explained that although she'd pledged a sorority in college, it'd been dedicated to public service.

"I'll never forget the first time I saw Becky," Lisa was saying.

Isabelle's ears perked up.

"She was in the sorority house dining room folding the napkins into pink butterflies. She was so"—Lisa searched for the word, the wine having stunted her vocabulary—"creative."

"You knew Becky in college? She was in your sorority?"

"Not *in* it, not at first. She was working her way through school waiting on table. That's what they called it back then. Waiting on table."

"Becky was a waitress?"

"Didn't you read *Just Call Me Becky*? It was a number one best seller." Isabelle shook her head. "You don't know how it all started?" Another head shake. "Then let me tell you." She took another slurp of wine. "Becky came from a poor family. She couldn't afford to pay for college, much less sorority dues. So she made money any way she could—waited on table, worked in the library, did alterations on clothes. She was a tip-top seamstress.

"When I met her, she was a junior like me. And she was working in the dining room, but she wasn't just going to *work* there. She also wanted to make it nicer. Before long, she was helping us fix up the house, make it homey and sweet. And eventually, she got to be a full-fledged member, even though she couldn't pay the dues. The girls voted her in unanimously and free of charge."

"Wow," Isabelle said. "So you and Becky go way back."

Lisa swallowed a forkful of beef fried rice. "We sure do. In fact, it was a few of us from the house who started Becky's very first business, catering teas and luncheons on campus. But Becky was always in charge. She was the one who had the drive. Even back then she wanted things to be just so. She had so much style—she always knew what was the right thing to do or say or wear, the right way to tie a scarf or write a thank-you note."

"Has she changed much since then?"

Lisa thought about it. Since her brain function was somewhat slowed, it took her a while.

"Hmm . . . not really. It's just that now everything's *bigger*, you know?"

"I'm not sure I understand."

"I mean, in school, if she wanted to splurge on a present for herself, she'd buy a pretty hair bow. Now she buys a jet and decorates it so it's just perfect. And back then there was a little group of us that wanted to be just like her. Now everybody does. Thousands of people read her magazine and try to live like she does because they know it'll make them superhappy. Everyone wants to work for her, to be part of the BBM family. Just so long as you see things the way she does, everything's jolly. Right?"

Lisa's smile, though sloppy, seemed genuine. If she was being the least bit ironic, Isabelle couldn't see it.

"Are there many other people from that original group who still work at BBM?"

"Oh, no," Lisa said. "Just me. The others got married or moved on to other things. They never really understood Becky's vision like I did. I'm her best and oldest friend at the company. We're like sisters."

Lisa smiled again, this time in a way that made Isabelle think the woman needed a pile of Prozac. It occurred to her that not once in the time she'd been working at BBM had Becky met with Lisa, or so much as called her.

"I bet you had no idea what an important person you're working for," Lisa continued. "And wait until Becky sees what a terrific book we're putting together for her. She's going to be *thrilled*!"

Isabelle stayed at Lisa's all day and actually had a good time. Her boss might be a self-indulgent nut, she decided, but she was a well-intentioned nut. After lunch, when the apartment got hot despite the air-conditioning, Lisa offered to lend her a bathing suit so they could take a dip in the building's rooftop pool. They splashed around for half an hour, while the teenage lifeguard read *Maxim* and Sprinkles ran impassioned laps around the deck.

As she floated on her back, the excess material of the one-piece swimsuit giving her an impromptu breast enlargement, Isabelle reflected that maybe her life didn't suck so much, after all. Here she was, swimming high above Manhattan, with the city looking golden and lovely in the sunlight. If she hadn't landed her dream job, at least she was gainfully employed and in no immediate danger of starvation. She'd recently avoided marrying a self-centered jerk and had just had two great dates with a guy who appeared to be both straight and single. If she could only make enough at the diner to afford cable TV, maybe life would be worth living.

After toweling off to Sprinkles' maniacal yapping, they went downstairs and worked for another four hours. By eight, Isabelle was once again ready to strangle her boss.

It wasn't that the assignment was hard—at least it wouldn't be if Lisa didn't insist on second-guessing every decision, until she'd remade each page in her mocked-up book at least four times. At nine, Isabelle knew she had to either make a graceful exit or impale herself on a glue stick. Pleading exhaustion, she promised Lisa she'd come back at seven a.m. and walked home.

It took visions of another rooftop swim to get her out of bed the next morning; the thought of messing around with Lisa's pet project made her want to pull the covers over her head. Still, she got out the door by quarter to seven and even stopped to pick up coffee and bagels for both of them.

The doorman, who recognized her from the day before, waved her in. But when she got to Lisa's apartment, there was no one home. She rang the bell three times, to no avail; she couldn't even hear Lisa's rat dog barking on the other side of the door. Figuring she'd probably taken him for a walk, Isabelle sat in the hall and waited: ten minutes, twenty, half an hour. She drank her coffee and ate her bagel, then started eyeing Lisa's.

Eventually, she decided to go to the office; it'd be just like Lisa to change her plans without telling her. She got into the elevator and was about to push the button for the lobby when she pushed Roof instead; it would also be just like Lisa to go for a swim and lose track of time.

As soon as she got off the elevator, she knew she'd made the right call; she could hear the dog yapping. She followed the sound down the hall and through the glass door that led to the pool. There was no one in the lounge chairs—no surprise, since it was early, and Lisa had told her that most of her neighbors had decamped to the Hamptons to escape the city heat.

And sure enough, there was her boss, who'd been lolling in the pool while Isabelle sat outside her apartment like a frustrated Jehovah's Witness. She opened her mouth to make a smart remark when something stopped her.

It was the fact that Lisa was floating facedown.

isabelle's first instinct on seeing Lisa floating in the pool had been to dive in and rescue her; that's what they taught you in Junior Lifesaving. So she'd kicked off her sandals, shed the top layer of her sweater set, and sprung off the concrete into the water. She made it to Lisa's side in two even strokes and turned her over on her back, surprised at how automatically the training had kicked in. She put an arm around Lisa's neck and floated her to the shallow end, pushing her hair back in preparation for mouth-to-mouth.

But then everything derailed: the sight of Lisa's face was so off, so wrong, that it snapped Isabelle out of lifesaving mode. She backed away from the body, now floating faceup in the water, brownish-black hair undulating, acting like it had a mind of its own.

Until that moment, it hadn't occurred to Isabelle that Lisa might actually be dead. Maybe it was because everything happened so fast. But when she turned her over and saw those empty brown eyes, it came as a shock. She backed up until she hit the wall of the pool and pulled herself out of the water. When she stood up, she was dripping wet, hair in her face and khaki slacks clinging. Still on autopilot, she looked around for a towel and found one tossed next to a plastic goblet and a bottle of white wine. It was only after she'd dried herself off as best she could that she realized that the towel, as well as the wine, must have belonged to Lisa.

Isabelle was halfway back to the elevator when she stopped, an odd sense of duty competing with her desire to get the hell out of there. She couldn't just leave Lisa like that, could she? It seemed gross, disloyal. Wouldn't it be better to take her out of the pool—wasn't that the least she could do? She walked back to the water's edge and tried to psych herself into diving back in, but she couldn't do it; the idea of touching Lisa's sad, waterlogged body was too revolting. Her face was soft, almost waxlike, on its way to ruin. *She's been here all night*, Isabelle thought. And although she wasn't quite sure how she knew this, it struck her as the truth.

The dog, for his part, seemed to disapprove of Isabelle's cowardice. He kept barking his yippy bark, looking at Isabelle as if to say that if she were a decent human being, she'd be able to get Lisa to stand up and give him a biscuit and make everything right with the world. She turned her back on him and headed toward the elevator, but once again her conscience got to her. This time she picked up the wriggling little dog and carried him under her arm all the way down to the lobby, where she told the doorman to call 911.

.   .   .

Not having worked for a big company before, Isabelle didn't have a feel for office politics, for the human dynamics that develop when you put three thousand people inside a building where the windows don't open. If she had, she might have anticipated what happened next.

As it was, she was thoroughly unprepared for her new status at Becky Belden Multimedia: martyr of the moment. Everyone in the building suddenly knew who she was. The area outside Lisa's office, which had always been as boring as a nun's confession, became a way station for all manner of well-wishers, condolence-givers, and the unabashedly curious. People brought Isabelle flowers and snacks, stopped by to say they were sorry, but mostly they just wanted to hear the story. Isabelle was sick of telling it—just explaining it to the cops had been bad enough—and she'd taken to implying that reliving it all was just too much for her.

By midafternoon, her e-mail in-box was overflowing with offers of coffee and a sympathetic ear. All the attention had started when a human resources executive named Jeffrey Bing—the same one who'd been so pissed that Lisa had blown off the Japanese publishers' visit—stood up in front of a crowded conference room and announced that she had "passed on." He said the death had been ruled accidental, that grief counseling was available, and that since Lisa didn't have any immediate family, donations in her memory could be made to the North Shore Animal League. Oh, and one more thing: Lisa's dog needed a home.

Bing didn't say who'd found Lisa's body, but the rumors had started circulating soon enough. And after the first two dozen people had filtered by her desk like she was on exhibit at the Bronx Zoo, Isabelle decided it was time to go home. She was planning her exit when she overheard two women speculating about Lisa's replacement. Would it be somebody from the department, or would they recruit a heavy hitter from the outside?

"Bet they bring in someone new," the first woman said. "Probably want to re-org the whole department. Becky likes to keep things fresh, recruit top talent. That gal sure knows what she's about."

The two kept walking, leaving Isabelle to wonder if they were right. Was special projects really going to be reorganized? What would that mean for her? And was there anything she could do that might be—she grappled for a word she'd seen in self-help books—proactive? Was there someone she could talk to?

The first person who came to mind, of course, was Mac Collins. But as quickly as Isabelle thought of asking him, she dismissed the idea. Her relationship with Mac was weird enough as it was.

Figuring she might as well prepare for the worst, she looked up the company's internal job postings online. The pickings were slim: an art director position at the magazine, some sort of regulatory compliance job in H.R., a computer gig in tech support. She was totally unqualified for all of them.

Her phone rang, an unusual occurrence even when Lisa was alive. She let it ring five times, because she wasn't sure what to say.

"Lisa K—er . . . special projects. Isabelle speaking."

"Isabelle, this is Bill Friedrich. I hope I'm not disturbing you."

She tried to place the name and the voice; she knew she'd heard them both before, but for the life of her, she couldn't remember where.

"Um, no. You're not disturbing me."

"We've only met briefly, but after what's happened, I wanted to express my condolences. It can't be easy for you."

"Thank you," Isabelle said. "That's very kind." She was still trying to figure out who he was. Friedrich. Where had she heard that name before? "I, uh . . . Were you a friend of Lisa's?"

"A colleague," he said. "We worked together on a number of occasions."

"Oh. Well, it's really sweet of you to call."

"I wanted to make sure you were aware of our employee counseling services. If you need someone to talk to, feel free to go to the Friendship Center. Or if that makes you uncomfortable, you can do it by phone."

"Thanks. I'll definitely think about it."

"Good," he said. "Remember, Becky wouldn't want you to go it alone."

She was about to go home when she got another e-mail, which she assumed was more condolences; she was going to blow it off until the next day, but then she recognized the name. It reminded her, as if she needed reminding, that Lisa wasn't the only denizen of the special projects team to wind up in the morgue.

chapter 14

Dear Miss Leonard,

*Sorry it took me so long to get back to you but our server's
been crashed and I just got your message. If you don't mind,
I would really like that picture of me and Marcia. I'd ask
you to mail it but I'm afraid it'd get lost so is it okay if I
come by your office sometime and pick it up?*

Thanks very much—

Jim Simons

It was Marcia Landon's boyfriend, whose e-mail address
Isabelle had found during her late-night raid on the downstairs
storage room. The memory felt foreign, like it had happened a
long time ago instead of a week. The whole scene made her feel
embarrassed—the way she'd made so much out of so little,
turning a silly errand into a major melodrama. After what she'd
seen in the swimming pool, she felt like a moron for hiding

behind a stack of files just because a couple of guys were moving some boxes.

She wrote back to Jim, suggesting they meet in the park across from BBM whenever he had time. Then she skimmed the other e-mails, wondering whether politeness required her to respond, and finally decided she didn't have the energy.

Although Isabelle could've justified taking the subway—finding one's boss dead at seven-thirty in the morning seemed an excellent excuse for self-pampering—she decided to walk. She thought the streets of New York might help her get the vision of Lisa's half-melted face out of her head, that the legions of commuters and hucksters and cops could act as some sort of mental emetic. She was halfway home when she realized that it was the first time she'd ever actually craved the city—that right at that moment, she'd rather be there than anywhere else, including home.

Isabelle wasn't sure what it said about her that it took a tragedy to make her feel like she belonged in Manhattan, if only for thirty blocks. Come to think of it, she wasn't sure what it said about the city, either.

. . .

Jeffrey Bing had been either discreet or simply clueless. The *New York Post* was neither.

Isabelle went out for the paper first thing the next morning—which, considering that she couldn't sleep, meant five-thirty a.m. She'd wanted to see if the *Times* had covered Lisa's death, but the *Post*'s headline was irresistible: IN THE DRINK: INEBRIATED UPPER EAST SIDE EXEC DIES IN POSH ROOFTOP POOL.

There was a picture of Lisa, grainy and not particularly recent, along with a story about how she'd drowned. It talked about how her blood alcohol level had been well above the legal limit, and how the cops had found two empty bottles of wine in her apartment in addition to the one up by the pool. It quoted her neighbors as they tsk-tsked about her insistence on swimming after hours, how she'd been warned about it more than once. But she didn't listen—any more than she did when she was told that both pets and glass bottles were forbidden in the pool area.

As far as the paper was concerned, Lisa was an irresponsible lush who got what she deserved.

. . .

He walked into the diner at eight a.m., hours before she would've expected him. Isabelle saw him before he saw her, watched as he scanned the place for the tallish brunette in the polyester uniform. He looked uneasy, out of place; for the first time in her experience, Mac Collins looked like he didn't know what he was doing.

He finally sat down at his usual booth, but when Isabelle came over, he stood up.

"I'm sorry," he said. "I . . ." He looked around the diner as though he could get some inspiration from the scruffy guy at the counter, a regular who was trying to chase off his hangover with a double order of sausage. "It's early."

"I know. You're usually not here till one or so."

"Anyway . . . I should've come sooner."

"I only work here on weekends."

He shook his head. "I mean, I should've come to your office or your apartment. But I didn't know . . . I wasn't sure if it was the right thing to do."

"Why should you—"

"I wanted to make sure you were okay. After what happened

with Lisa..." His blue eyes were anxious, appealing for Isabelle's understanding. "I was afraid you might be..." He shook his head again, then rubbed the back of his neck. Out of nowhere, Isabelle had a vision of the boys who'd hung out in the corner at seventh-grade dances. "I don't know what I thought. But... are you okay?"

"Yeah," Isabelle said. "I mean, it was awful. And I haven't exactly been sleeping. But I guess I'm all right."

"Listen, I'm sorry I didn't come by before. I wasn't sure I should barge in. And to be honest, I was—"

"Let me guess. Busy."

He cracked a hint of a smile. "Right."

"Do you want to sit down? I mean... can you stay?"

"Yeah," he said. "I can stay."

He sat down, and when it came time to order, he asked her to bring him anything. She opted for the French toast, which Mrs. Mendes made with cardamom and vanilla.

"So," he said when she delivered it, "after your shift, do you want to get some air?"

"Are you sure you're up to it? You look tired."

"You're the one who hasn't been sleeping."

"True."

"You want to talk about it?" He doused his toast in syrup, keeping his eyes on his plate. Isabelle got the feeling he was trying to sound casual.

"Talk about what?" She took an interest in her order pad.

"Lisa. Finding her like that."

"No."

He gave a low whistle. "Okay, then."

"I'd rather just go out and do something. Take my mind off it."

"What are you in the mood for?"

"Well . . . you ever seen the Rockettes?"

His expression turned horrified. "Not *that*."

She smiled at him. After the grimness of the past few days, she was surprised her face remembered how. "Don't worry. They're not playing right now. I checked."

"Phew."

"Have you ever been to Jackson Heights?"

"Queens? Not recently. Why?"

"I hear there's a ton of Indian stores there, and you can go around and try different things—like get a meat samosa here and a vegetable pakora there. Lots of Indian bakeries, too."

"And what would we do after that—assuming we haven't died of ptomaine?"

"We'd walk it off."

"Walk where?"

"Home."

"From *Queens*?"

"Well, as far as we could. We could always hop on the subway if we get tired."

"Isabelle Leonard," he said, "you are utterly out of your mind."

She tried not to wonder what he meant by that as they wandered in and out of narrow storefronts sampling pakora and papadum and other things they'd never even heard of. When they were too full to eat one more milk sweet, they started walking—and walking, and walking, until the strap broke on one of Isabelle's Italian sandals and Mac hailed a gypsy cab.

They both got out at Isabelle's building; she told him he could go home, but he said no gentleman leaves a lady to hop up to her apartment on one foot. When they got to her front door, she stood there with her shoe in her hand and thanked him for a great afternoon. No, he said, he was the one who was grateful; once again she'd made him see the city in a different way.

It was all very polite, Isabelle thought, wondering how long he was going to stand there. Was she supposed to shake his hand? Finally, when she was starting to get uncomfortable, he said something.

"Can I come in?"

"Oh, God, no."

She'd said it before she could stop herself, and he didn't take it well. His face hardened, and he started to turn in the direction of the elevator.

"Sorry," he said over his shoulder. "I shouldn't have asked."

"No, wait," she said, taking two big strides and grabbing his arm. "That's not what I meant. It's not you, it's . . . it's me."

He looked down at her, a rueful smile on his face. "*There's* a line a guy's never heard before."

"No, I mean it. It's not that I don't want you to come in. I do. It's just that—"

"I know. You're upset about Lisa. I shouldn't have asked."

"It's not that. It's—"

"Come on, you can skip the consolation speech. I'm a big boy."

"Jesus Christ," she said, "I'm telling you the truth. I really do want to invite you in."

"Then what's the—"

"I don't have any furniture."

"What?"

"When my ex left, I kind of lost my mind and gave all his stuff to the Salvation Army. My apartment's totally empty except for a futon and a couple of milk crates."

He still seemed perplexed. Then he just said, "Oh."

"So you can understand why I don't want to advertise it."

"It's nothing to be ashamed of."

"Spoken like a man who owns a goddamn footstool."

"Honestly," he said, "I really don't care. I just wanted to, uh"—he fumbled over the words—"to see you for a little while longer. I don't care if we sit on the floor."

"That's pretty much what it would amount to."

He gestured toward the door. "Then lead the way."

chapter 15

She undid the lock, still feeling uncomfortable—both about Mac seeing the vast wasteland that was her apartment and about what might happen once they got in there. "Sorry I can't offer you anything to drink," she said. "I don't have any . . . Wait, maybe I do."

She headed for the bathroom, extracted a half-empty bottle of Knob Creek from the cabinet under the sink, and brought it into the living room along with her battered radio. "I just came across it a couple of days ago," she said. "My ex must've left it there—don't ask me what it was doing in the john."

He went into the kitchen and poured himself two fingers on the rocks. Then he joined her on the floor, backs against the living room wall, and for the next few minutes the two of them sat there listening to Ella Fitzgerald singing, of all things, "I'll Take Manhattan."

"Isabelle," he said finally, "that guy was one stupid son of a bitch."

"Nice of you to say so."

"Does he ever come sniffing around?"

Isabelle rolled her eyes. "Hell no. God forbid he should be reminded of how he almost lowered himself to marry a girl from the wrong side of the tracks."

He propped himself up on one elbow, balancing the drink on his knee. "Is that really how you see yourself?"

"No," she said, "but that's how he saw me. And at first, I think he got a kick out of it—like I was his personal charity project. He used to say I was his 'diamond in the rough.'" She shook her head at the memory. "His family definitely didn't approve—which was probably part of the appeal in the first place. But when push came to shove, he bolted."

"I'm sorry."

"Yeah, well, I'm not. If he hadn't, I'd be married to the creep."

"At least then you'd have a footstool," he said, deadpan.

"So . . . what about you? Any major heartbreaks?"

He thought about it. "No major ones. Not even many minor ones."

"How'd you manage that?"

"Hell," he said, "I don't know. I guess I've always dated a certain kind of woman."

"And what kind is that?"

"The sophisticated kind that enjoys an expensive dinner and a pleasant roll in the hay without a lot of complications."

"Hmm. You know, I've never actually met that kind of woman. I think she only exists in the minds of men."

"You just haven't been in the city long enough."

"Yeah," she said, "I get that a lot."

. . .

The kiss didn't take her entirely by surprise. Something in his eyes predicted it, although she had to admit that when it was over, he seemed astounded by what he'd just done. One minute they'd been talking about her idiot ex-fiancé, the next he was putting down his glass and wrapping one arm around her shoulders and pressing his mouth to hers.

Isabelle had wondered what kind of kisser he'd be, whether he'd be gentle or aggressive, and in the end she decided he was just the right mixture of both. The kiss lasted a long time, but there was no groping whatsoever; although he drew her body in close to his, something in the way he held her made it clear this wasn't foreplay.

Still, if Mac had himself under control, Isabelle got the feeling it was tenuous. If she'd decided to let herself go—to give in to how incredibly good it felt to be touched by another human being—she had a feeling she could sweep him away . . . and directly onto her futon.

But she didn't try, and neither did he. Once they'd pulled apart, Mac looked awkward but not unhappy; when Isabelle wondered what she herself must look like, the first word that came to mind was *carnivorous*.

They'd sat there talking for a while longer, neither one of them commenting on what had happened. He finished his drink, said it was time he got going, and did. By way of a good-night kiss, he pecked her on the cheek.

·   ·   ·

If Isabelle hadn't known that Jim Simons was a "software specialist," she probably would've guessed. The guy was a computer nerd right out of central casting, with his white short-sleeved sport shirt and no-iron khakis and geeky glasses and cathode-ray pallor. He was soft, too, not only in the middle but all over, and Isabelle recalled that he'd looked more fit in the photograph. Maybe Marcia had been a good influence on him.

Isabelle had been waiting for him in the park for twenty minutes. She'd only heard back from him that morning, a Monday whose sky was heavy with the threat of rain. He'd sent her a note laden with more apologies about his e-mail server—which, as far as she could see, didn't bode well for whatever high-tech company he worked for.

"You must be Jim," she said, standing up when she saw him approach her bench.

"Yeah, uh . . . How did you know?"

"I've seen your picture."

He reddened a little. "Right."

"You want to sit down?" He nodded and sat next to her on the bench. She expected him to ask for the photo, but he didn't say anything, just stared down at his unlaced right sneaker. "So," she said finally, "like I said in the e-mail, I found this in my desk."

She pulled an envelope out of her purse and offered it to him. He took it, opened it, bit his bottom lip.

"I've never seen this one before," he said. "Other ones from the same roll, but not this one." He stared at the picture, then cleared his throat like it might help him not cry. "Did you know Marcia?"

Isabelle shook her head. "No, but everybody told me how nice she was. Everybody really misses her a lot." Isabelle knew she was exaggerating, but it seemed like the thing to do.

Jim stared at the picture some more. "Can you imagine how horrible it must've been?" Isabelle wasn't sure what he meant, so she didn't answer. Eventually, he shifted his gaze to his other sneaker and said, "Dying like that."

"I can't imagine."

He cleared his throat again, but it didn't help; when he turned to look at Isabelle, his eyes were all teary.

"I didn't believe her. I said she was being melodramatic."

"About what?"

"About the fact," he said, "that someone was trying to kill her."

chapter 16

"**are you serious?**"

"No," Jim said, swiping at his eyes. "I'm joking. Isn't it fucking funny?"

"I'm sorry, I . . . I guess I don't get it."

"No, you don't. I didn't, either. And I should've believed her, too. Marcia didn't have any family left. Her friends and I— we were all she had."

"But I don't understand. I thought . . . Everybody says she was killed by some crazy homeless man."

"I know that's what they say. And maybe he did kill her—he confessed, anyway. At first, he denied it, but then he admitted it and they sent him away to some hospital somewhere. But that doesn't change what happened before, the way I treated her."

Jim fumbled in his pants pocket, and Isabelle thought he was going to smoke, but he pulled out a pack of gum. He popped two pieces from the plastic sheet and threw them into his mouth, an oddly violent gesture. Isabelle watched his jaw muscles work as he chewed.

"You have to understand," he said. "Marcia and I were totally like opposites attract, you know? I was the serious one, she was the character. She had this really big personality, and it drove me crazy sometimes." He glanced at Isabelle, an alarmed look on his face. "Don't get me wrong. I really loved her. I still do. But I guess what I mean to say is, Marcia always made a lot out of everything. If she found a quarter on the sidewalk, it was like she won the lottery. And if the Chinese place she liked was out of sesame noodles, it was like her heart was broken. She just . . . Like one of her friends said at the funeral, she lived life across the whole spectrum. You understand?"

"I think so."

He shook his head. "I'm probably totally boring you. Nobody wants to hear about somebody else's problems. They pretend they do, but they don't."

"No, I'm really interested." When he turned to skewer her with another glance, she added, "Honestly, I am. I mean, I sit in her chair, okay? I'm curious about what kind of person she was."

"You don't have to get back to work?"

"It's okay."

He took a deep breath. "So, like I said, Marcia was pretty good at making something out of nothing—not in a bad way, not like she was being malicious or anything, more like she just liked being the center of attention. So when . . . stuff started to happen, she made a big deal out of it. I thought she was just being paranoid."

"What started to happen, exactly?"

"Weird things, accidents. Like she had this garden on the fire escape. You're not supposed to, but she did. She hung out there a lot when the weather was good. She'd sit out and read for hours. And one day the railing broke—it just snapped, and she almost fell off."

"And she thought somebody broke it on purpose?"

"Not then, not at first. But then she had this other close call. She was on her way to work one morning when a big slab of concrete from a construction site came crashing down next to her—it only missed her by a couple of feet."

"And she thought it wasn't an accident?"

"Between that and what happened with the fire escape, she went a little nuts."

"Did she go to the police?"

He shook his head. "She wanted to. I told her they'd think she was crazy."

"What about after she was . . . after it happened?"

"I tried. But like I said, the guy confessed. Case closed."

"And was there, you know, any evidence or anything? For those two other times?"

"The landlord said the fire escape was just old, and he fixed it really fast and gave her a free month's rent—I think he was afraid of getting sued. And as for the other thing, the city cited the contractor. That was the end of it."

"But she was still afraid?"

"Yeah. She thought someone was out to get her—like she was doomed or something. Marcia was a big believer in fate."

"And now you think she was right?"

"She's dead," he said. "What am I supposed to think?"

chapter 17

isabelle took the subway to work the next morning, because she was running way behind. She'd spent way too much time getting herself dressed, trying on outfit after outfit, leaving the rejects in a tangle on her bed.

What was a "production assistant" supposed to wear? And, come to think of it, what was a production assistant supposed to *do*? All Isabelle had been told was that she was no longer an employee of special projects; from now on, she'd be working behind the scenes on *The Becky Belden Show*.

When she'd heard the news, she was afraid they'd mixed her up with someone else. Why had she been chosen to work on one of the most successful shows on daytime TV? Despite her curiosity, Isabelle was afraid to ask; God forbid the powers-that-be should come to their senses and put her out of a job. And if there actually had been a mix-up, Isabelle was determined to impress her bosses so much that by the time they figured it out, they'd want to keep her on, anyway.

That was part of the motivation behind Isabelle's seven

a.m. fashion show. She'd seen the assistants running around before the taping she'd watched, and they'd seemed so hip in their low-slung black pants and cropped turtleneck sweaters and interesting eyeglasses. But Isabelle didn't own any clothes like theirs. What she still had from her old life was more crunchy-granola than anything else, and the stuff Laurence had paid for made her look like the ad executive's wife she'd so narrowly missed becoming.

When she got to the Belden Building, she headed for the special entrance she'd used to watch the taping two weeks before. She showed the guard at the door her new ID, walked through an empty lobby, and wandered around in search of someone to tell her what to do. Finding no one, she went back out and asked the guard if he knew where everyone was.

"It's Tuesday," he said. "They got their regular nine o'clock meeting. Upstairs conference room."

She followed his directions up a staircase and down the hall—toward the voices she heard coming out an open door. She poked her head in, trying to be unobtrusive. Becky Belden was at the front of the room, leading a crowd of about two dozen people in some sort of chant.

"We are just vessels," she said.

Everyone repeated it. *We are just vessels.*

"People's stories flow through us."

People's stories flow through us.

"We take pleasure and pride in sharing their inspirational tales with the world."

We take pleasure and pride in . . .

It went on like that for a while, Becky spouting inspirational slogans and her audience repeating them. They all had their eyes closed, and they were holding hands; the scene reminded Isabelle of the fundamentalist Christian kids who used to pray around the high school flagpole every morning. They were always so well scrubbed and cheery, and they scared the hell out of her.

Becky and her followers finished with a mantra about how they hoped this week's shows would bring joy to their viewing public. Then everyone gathered around a table in the corner and started serving themselves from carafes of coffee and baskets of muffins. Isabelle wasn't sure if she should join them; she lingered in the doorway until a tall African American woman asked what she was doing.

"I'm the new production assistant," she said. "Isabelle Leonard."

"We're not expecting a new P.A.," the woman said.

"Um, human resources said I was supposed to come here." Isabelle waved her new badge for emphasis. "They said I was supposed to start work on the show today."

The woman let out an aggrieved sigh, then put out a hand. "I'm Leslie Peters, one of the associate producers. Grab a chair and a muffin and sit in on the meeting. After, I'll get somebody to show you around."

The meeting lasted an hour and consisted mostly of the producers going over the topics for that week's shows and brainstorming ideas for future episodes. They talked about the logistical details of keeping certain guests apart until the proper on-air moment, and last-minute research to make sure each episode was as up-to-date as possible. When they were done, one producer presented plans for a special holiday episode of *At Home with Becky,* her popular lifestyle program;

another discussed the schedule for *Becky Belden's Food 'n' Friends,* her new cooking show that featured guest chefs, a studio audience, and phone calls from starstruck fans.

Becky sat there and nodded throughout the meeting, but she didn't say much. From what Isabelle could tell, she didn't actually *do* much, either. Maybe she'd been naive, but it had never occurred to her that Becky Belden didn't come up with her own topics, or choose her own guests, or even write her own questions. But the longer she sat there, the more Isabelle got the feeling that the only thing Becky Belden did on her own TV programs was show up.

When the meeting was over, Leslie introduced Isabelle to a woman about her own age. Her name was Brynna, and Isabelle realized she'd already met her; she was the one who'd come by her desk to scare up extra audience members.

"You ever been a P.A. before?"

"No," Isabelle said, trailing her as she trotted down the hall.

"Okay, it's like this," Brynna said. "You're a peon."

"Excuse me?"

"You're a slave. An indentured servant. Anything anybody tells you to do, you do. If you have bright, creative ideas, keep them to yourself. And if you work hard enough, and never screw up, maybe you'll get to be an assistant producer someday."

"Really? So . . . what do I do first?"

"First," she said, "you can go fix the stopped-up toilet in the guests' dressing room."

Isabelle thought she was kidding—until the girl handed her a plunger. The job took her half an hour, at the end of which she was covered in sweat and God knows what else. Then she was put to work filling the audience's gift sacks for the entire week—twenty-five hundred silver bags stuffed with samples of bubble bath and room spray and women's nutrition bars. At noon, she was the one who got sent down to the commissary to bring back the food; one of the fringe benefits of working on *The Becky Belden Show*, she learned, was that lunch was provided. It didn't take her long to figure out the reason: everyone was way too busy to go out.

At showtime, Isabelle wasn't allowed backstage; since she didn't know what she was doing, Brynna said she'd just get in the way. Her job was to be a "greeter," which meant that she stood outside the entrance to the studio and said, "Welcome to *The Becky Belden Show*," to each audience member as she handed out the gift bags.

She tried to keep a smile on her face as she welcomed the stragglers, but she was distracted. She could hear Mac inside the studio warming up the audience, and she was dying to go in and watch him. When they'd first met, Mac had told her that having him do it was one of Becky's "idiosyncrasies." And the more she got to know him, the more absurd it seemed—that a high-paid executive who was so busy he worked every weekend would spend his time telling one-liners to a bunch of tourists. But what Becky wanted, Becky got; Brynna had warned her about that even before she'd handed her the plunger.

"If any one of the producers asks you to do something, you do it, okay?" she'd said. "Even if it sounds impossible, don't even *think* about arguing with them. It just pisses them off."

"But they all seem so nice."

"Sure they are, most of the time. You just don't want to cross them."

"Cross them how?"

"Just never tell them no," she said, "and for chrissake, don't make any mistakes."

. . .

For chrissake, don't make any mistakes. The words haunted Isabelle for the next month, during which she worked so hard she was nostalgic for the spectacular boredom of special projects. All day she fetched and carried for the women who ran *The Becky Belden Show.* She'd come home so tired she'd barely be able to work on her latest stab at fiction, a sci-fi adventure she was concocting about a busty space princess and an army of invading robots. And though she'd hoped that her new job might help her make some contacts in the publishing world, so far she hadn't even been allowed backstage while the show was taping. No, she only got to plunge toilets, get coffee, and hand out gift bags to the Becky-obsessed tourists.

As she stretched out in the bathtub, one encounter stuck out in her mind as particularly humiliating. She'd been distributing free samples of tooth-whitening strips for a taping of "Makeover Monday," one of the show's most popular features, when an elderly woman in a blue velour jumpsuit asked her for directions to the ladies' room. Isabelle told her, whereupon the woman hugged her, rhapsodizing about how wonderful it must be to work for Becky—and how, if Isabelle was lucky, maybe someday Becky would be kind enough to give *her* a makeover, too.

The idea that some dowdy midwesterner thought she needed a makeover made Isabelle sink lower into the water, which was deliciously hot and filled with jasmine-scented bubbles. The radio was set to Isabelle's favorite country station, which played a satisfying assortment of tunes about spunky women and the men who done them wrong. Baths, at least, were one pleasure Isabelle hadn't had to give up.

As she lathered herself with a pink scrubby, her thoughts

returned to their usual perch: Mac Collins. They'd seen each other every Saturday, gone on excursions to Ellis Island and Harlem and Yankee Stadium, but so far their relationship hadn't evolved beyond a series of high-octane good-night kisses.

It was beginning to drive her insane.

The image of Mac—particularly, she admitted, his very attractive rear end—made the water temperature seem higher, although Isabelle knew it had to be cooling down. Why hadn't he made a more aggressive move? And, come to think of it, why didn't she ever hear from him at work? She'd wondered whether there was some rule against fraternization, but she hadn't checked. In her more paranoid moments, she worried that maybe he was living a double life—that he had an elegant, Wellesley-bred girlfriend during the week and was just using Isabelle for cheap thrills on the weekend. But, she reflected, since he hadn't sought much in the way of thrills, her theory didn't make much sense.

Men, she thought. *And they think we're difficult. So far this summer, one guy has ditched me at the altar, and another has me so confused I don't know which way is up.*

Isabelle let out some water and turned on the hot tap. She poured in more jasmine bubbles and lay back, knowing she needed to shave her legs but feeling too tired to bother. At least she ought to fix her toenail polish, which was getting so old it'd left hot-pink flakes inside her shoes.

Later, Isabelle wasn't sure which subject distracted her enough so she didn't hear him. Was it Mac, her legs, the toenail polish? Or was the man so adept at breaking into apartments, even those in fancy Upper East Side doorman buildings like hers, that it wouldn't have made any difference?

Whatever the answer, the net result was that Isabelle Leonard was lying blissfully in the bathtub, soaking in the hot water and the bubbles that smelled like jasmine, when she suddenly realized she was going to die.

chapter 18

The man was dressed like a parody of a cat burglar—all in black, even gloves and a ski mask. It was such a stereotype, in fact, that for a split second, Isabelle thought she was dreaming. She'd been dozing off when something alerted her. She opened her eyes and there he was, a ninja-clad stranger invading her bathroom. She had time to open her mouth to scream, but not enough for any sound to come out. The man took two steps toward her, but just when Isabelle thought he was going to put his hands on her, he grabbed the antiquated boom box instead. She watched it travel toward the tub with what seemed like exaggerated slowness, as though it knew what would happen when it hit the water and was in no hurry to get there.

When it finally did, Isabelle got a shock and then a *shock*.

The first came amid a shower of sparks and an acrid smell, and it made her jump out of the water like an extremely graceless porpoise.

The second was metaphorical: it was the illogical, unexpected understanding that she wasn't dead.

For a second, the intruder seemed as confused as she was. Time stalled as they stood there staring at each other, Isabelle dripping wet and utterly disoriented. Then, just as she was starting to gird herself for his next attack, he turned and ran. She heard him pause in the living room—why she didn't know—then take off out the door and down the hall.

The sound of the heavy door slamming snapped Isabelle back to full consciousness, though not quite to her senses. Fueled by instinct and adrenaline, she flew out of the apartment and into the hall as the black-clad man was turning the corner toward the fire stairs. He never looked back at her, just kept up a greyhound's pace down the steps, unencumbered by whatever it was he had tucked under his arm. He kept widening his lead as Isabelle raced down the five flights after him, so by the time she made it to the lobby, he'd already gone out the front entrance and disappeared. She stood in front of her building looking frantically left and right, but there was no sign of him, not even any clue which direction he'd gone. *Goddammit.*

"Miss Leonard?"

It was Patrick, one of the building's squadron of well-mannered Irish doormen. He was looking at her with an expression that in her state of half-delirium struck her as quite complicated—a mixture of confusion, concern, and . . . appreciation.

It was at that point, and not a moment earlier, that Isabelle realized she was stark naked.

She made a comical effort to cover herself, and he wrapped her in the epauletted navy-blue jacket that Isabelle had always thought made him look like he was crewing the Love Boat. She mumbled something about how her apartment had been broken into, how a man had tried to kill her and she'd chased him downstairs, and once she was back in her apartment and wearing a bathrobe, he called 911.

. . .

The two uniformed cops who came to Isabelle's apartment weren't mean or especially incompetent, but they didn't inspire confidence. This was a major disappointment to Isabelle, who in addition to being a recent crime victim was a longtime fan of police dramas in which the good guys invariably got their man in sixty minutes, including commercials.

But the officers who occupied Isabelle's living room that Wednesday night didn't hold out much hope that her attacker would be caught. One of them—a redhead whose hair was so severely French-braided Isabelle thought she looked like she'd had Botox—seemed irritated that Isabelle had given them so little to go on. There were no fingerprints, not even a description beyond the fact that Isabelle thought he was about five foot ten and had a wiry build.

The officers spent a great deal of time telling her that this was probably just the latest in a string of burglaries on the Upper East Side. The perp, as they called him, no doubt thought there was no one home; when he found her in the tub, he'd panicked and thrown the radio at her. It was lucky for her that the apartment had been rewired with safety switches, so all she got was a nasty shock.

"But why would a burglar even go into the bathroom?" Isabelle asked. "It's not like there's anything valuable in there."

"In this city," the male cop said, "people put things in places you wouldn't believe."

"But there was something about him . . . ," Isabelle began, then stopped. The cops looked at her like she was keeping them from their dinner. "It was like . . . there was something familiar about him."

The policeman summoned up something resembling interest. "You think you know him?"

"I don't know. There was just something familiar, that's all."

"Do you think you could ID him?"

"I . . . No."

They asked her if anything had been stolen, and Isabelle told them that although she thought the man had had something under his arm, she didn't know what it was. It wasn't until they were about to leave that she realized what was missing: her laptop computer. That clinched it for the cops, who said they'd let her know if the Apple PowerBook was recovered, and walked out as though they were positive they'd never see her again. Then, in what was clearly the mother of all afterthoughts, one of them handed her a card for a victims' counseling hotline, which Isabelle promptly tossed in the trash.

Son of a bitch. Of all the things in her apartment—which, Isabelle had to admit, was basically nothing—the bastard had taken her laptop, her ticket out of wage slavery. Okay, so *Princess Astra and the Attack of the Fire Robots* wasn't going so well, but at least she'd written something that she hadn't immediately erased.

Isabelle realized her hands were shaking, and it wasn't just out of fury. She felt cold even with the heavy robe on, and she wondered whether she might be in mild shock. The cops had asked her if there was someone they could call to come keep her company, or better yet, someplace else she could spend the night, but she told them she was okay. Once they'd gone, though, she instantly felt a hundred times more vulnerable. The idea of going to sleep seemed preposterous, even with a hefty dose of Tylenol PM.

She checked the clock. It was one-thirty in the morning. Against her better judgment, and with hands shaking even more than before, she picked up the phone and dialed.

chapter 19

"Somebody tried to kill me tonight," she said.

The voice at the other end of the line was groggy, out of focus. "Is that the name of a song?"

"No, you idiot. Somebody broke into my apartment and threw the radio into the bathtub and almost killed me. So could you please—"

"Were you, like, *in* the bathtub at the time?"

"Of course, I was in it. What the hell do you think?"

That seemed to wake him up. "Oh my *God*." He cleared his throat. "You home still?"

"Yeah. The cops just left."

"You want to come down here and stay?"

"Hell no."

"I'll be there in half an hour."

Trevor was true to his word, showing up in under thirty minutes with a bouquet of daisies and a dime bag of something Isabelle wouldn't have smoked if she hadn't been so shaken up.

His first act after sitting on her futon was rolling her a joint roughly the size of her pinkie.

"What if my neighbors smell this?"

"Then we might have to share."

"And what if the cops come back to look for clues?"

"The NYPD? You must be joking."

She took a long drag, held the smoke in too long, and coughed. Isabelle, like many of her friends in Burlington, had indulged in her fair share of marijuana. But Laurence hadn't approved, and after swearing it off, she hadn't missed it. Now, though, she was glad for the way it was making her feel—like the whole world was a big joke and she was in on it.

Once he'd fashioned his own joint, Trevor wanted to know everything that'd happened. She recounted it in as much detail as she could remember. He seemed disappointed that the male cop hadn't been better looking, which struck Isabelle as a stupid thing to be fixated on at this particular moment. Finally, when the giant doobie was burned down to a stump and the bedroom chandelier was doing laps over her head, she asked him the question that had been weighing on her ever since the cops left.

"Trev," she said, dry mouth slurring her words, "why the hell do you think somebody wants me dead?"

He squinted at her, then his eyes popped comically wide. At least she thought they did; at the moment, she wasn't sure she could trust her senses, sight above all.

"Izzy, sweetheart, *no.*" Trevor shifted over to her side of the futon and put a clumsy arm around her. "Nobody wants to kill you, princess. I promise. You're safe as a . . . safe as a . . . *safe.*"

She shot up to a sitting position. "For chrissake, some guy broke into my apartment and tried to electrocute me. What the hell do you think he wanted?"

"It's like the cops said. He just wanted to rob the place, and when—"

"Bullshit."

"Listen, sweet pea, I know you're upset. Why don't you just—"

"What the hell is going on with this company?"

Isabelle shouted the words even louder than she'd meant to—and she'd meant to shout them pretty loud in the first place. Trevor's mouth fell open, but he didn't say anything.

The silence deflated her. She flopped back onto the futon, eyes filling with tears. Suddenly, Isabelle remembered why she'd never smoked dope all that often: she was the queen of the crying jag.

She lay there for a while—the drug, paradoxically, making the seconds seem engorged and the minutes truncated. When she finally spoke again, she wasn't even sure if Trevor was awake to hear her.

"Just listen to me, okay? Maybe I'm just a stupid hick who doesn't know what the hell she's doing, which is probably true. But just look at the facts. Look at the people who've died at BBM over the past six months. There's Marcia and Lisa and your friend and somebody else, and I think somebody after that, too, and then there's that guy who disappeared and they put his picture up all over the lobby. And now"—the tears popped out of her eyes and ran down her cheeks in fat, distinct rivulets—"now some son of a bitch wants to kill me, too. And I told you something was going on. I *told* you. But you didn't believe me. I told you about the boxes and the storeroom and those guys in there in the middle of the night, and you said I was a drama queen. But I'm not. Lisa's dead and Marcia's dead and what are the odds that both people who work in the same little department would end up dead? And now me!"

She was crying so hysterically she could barely breathe. Trevor made soothing shushing sounds as he patted her head and told her that it was okay, she was safe, nobody was out to get her.

"Don't worry, princess," he was saying in a voice only moderately more coherent than her own. "It's like I said before. It's a big company. Lots of things happen at a big company, because there's lots and lots of people for them to happen to. I know you're upset, but there's no big bad wolf out there trying to eat Little Red Riding Hood. I promise."

She opened one eye. "Really?"

"Really. This is all just an awful coincidence." Trevor smiled at her, an oversize grin obviously calculated to make her stop bawling. "BBM's just having a run of bad luck."

.   .   .

By the time she woke up sometime in the afternoon, Isabelle had no idea *what* she believed. She knew her mouth and throat felt like they'd been stuffed with Brillo pads, and she was absolutely starving. Beyond that, though, she was lost.

Trevor had left around nine that morning, promising to tell her boss on *The Becky Belden Show* that she was sick. He said he'd come by after work, and although Isabelle wasn't really in the mood to be alone, she wasn't much in the mood for company, either.

She dug through her cupboards in search of something to eat, coming up with Marshmallow Fluff, some old Triscuits, and what must've been Laurence's jar of martini olives. She leaned against the wall in the living room and slathered Fluff on the stale crackers, wishing she had some peanut butter to go with it.

Why had she called Trevor last night instead of Mac? She wasn't sure, but she thought it had something to do with her not wanting Mac to see her so vulnerable. But there was something else, she had to admit. Even though her relationship with Mac was starting to turn romantic, for some reason she trusted Trevor more. Maybe it was because of what she'd heard in the storeroom. Or because she and Trevor were equals, while Mac was an executive whose job she didn't begin to understand. And he wasn't just an executive at any company, but one where, as she herself had put it, the employees were dropping dead left and right.

Or were they? Was there really something sinister going on—what, Isabelle couldn't imagine—or was it just a coincidence, like Trevor said? What would the actuarial tables say about a half dozen people dying at a company of several thousand?

She'd once read an article about how the human mind naturally seeks out order amid chaos, imagining "cancer clusters" and celebrities dying in threes, when it was really just nature taking its course. Nature, as Tennyson put it, red in tooth and claw.

So what was going on? Was last night's break-in really a burglary gone awry? And who was the intruder? Why had he seemed familiar?

If the man had wanted to kill her, then why hadn't he? Isabelle had been entirely defenseless; he could have grabbed her, held her under the bathwater until she drowned. But he'd just taken her only valuable possession and run off—which, in the sensible light of day, made it seem like the cops knew what they were doing, after all.

And even if the cops didn't, she reflected, the burglar sure as hell did. He'd somehow picked the lock without leaving so much as a scratch, and he'd zeroed in on the only thing in the apartment that was worth anything. His only mistake had been entering the bathroom; if he hadn't, he could've made a clean getaway.

Which brought Isabelle back to her original conundrum. If the guy was such a pro, then why would he have made such a stupid mistake? Unless—Isabelle didn't want to let her mind go back there, but she couldn't help it—unless electrocuting her in the bathtub was his mission in the first place.

The buzz of the intercom nearly made her jump out of her pajamas. Her nerves were shot, no question about it; she felt the sweat soak the armpits of her T-shirt as she went to the speaker to answer. She also felt like an idiot: would her attacker really ring to ask if he could come up and have another go at frying her?

As it turned out, it was only the doorman—mercifully, not the same one who'd seen her running naked through the lobby—letting her know there was a package for her downstairs. Did she want him to bring it up? She said she did.

But once the box was sitting in her foyer, the events of the night before made her worry that maybe, just maybe, it might blow up in her face.

it wasn't ticking). That seemed a good sign.

Isabelle gave the box a tentative poke with her big toe. Not being blown to smithereens, she was emboldened to lean over and read the label. It had come via a courier service Isabelle had never heard of; the return address, to her utter confusion, was an electronics emporium downtown.

Can you mail-order a bomb from a regular store? Isabelle doubted it.

Curiosity trumping paranoia, she got a knife from the kitchen and sliced the sealing tape. Underneath the cardboard was a plethora of packing peanuts. Under those was yet another box, containing the newest, fastest, sexiest Apple laptop computer. Isabelle recognized it because she'd drooled on the picture in the MacMall catalog.

She dug through the box looking for a card or some other explanation, but all she found was a receipt that said the computer had been paid for in cash. It had cost more than Isabelle made in a month.

What was going on? Only a handful of people knew she'd lost her laptop the night before. The two cops sure hadn't bought her a new one, and Trevor couldn't afford it. That left the guy who stole it—and what were the odds that he'd decided that sending her a new computer was, in fact, preferable to killing her?

The receipt had the store's phone number on it; Isabelle called, but once she got through the touch-tone gauntlet, the voice at the other end said there was no way to trace a cash transaction. So much for her stab at detection.

Isabelle ran her hand across the top of the new laptop, sleek and metallic and pristine. She knew she ought to return it, but for the moment, she couldn't bring herself to pack it up. Feeling distinctly guilty, she uncoiled the power cord, plugged it in, and pushed the On button.

It was only then that it occurred to her that she'd just done something intensely stupid—that if there really *were* a bomb in there, maybe it was set to go off when she turned the computer on. Whether this was rational or the product of last night's terror was an open question; either way, it took her half a heartbeat to leap across the room and hide in the kitchen. She waited there for five minutes, crouched behind the counter, feeling increasingly idiotic.

Nothing exploded. Eventually, she ventured back into the living room. The laptop, still perched on top of the box, was welcoming her to the happy world of wireless computing.

She spent the evening fondling the computer and eating the Chinese takeout she'd ordered in a fit of residual self-pity from the events of the night before. Her pork fried rice and wonton soup came to nine dollars and change; she realized it was the most expensive meal she'd had since Laurence split. Or, she amended, the most expensive one she'd paid for herself, since Mac had paid for their dinners together.

Mac. Why hadn't she called him? Although he wasn't her boyfriend, they were definitely dating. Weren't they? So wasn't it appropriate that when some maniac broke into her apartment and tried to deep-fry her in her own bathtub, she'd give him a call?

She stared at the phone, feeling lonelier than she had since the morning after her aborted wedding, when she was supposed to be on a plane to Fiji, but instead wound up puking her guts out in a sparkling porcelain john at the Plaza Hotel.

She thought about calling Trevor, but she wasn't in the mood for his particular brand of company. So she just lay on her futon, the city lights illuminating her apartment as she tried to go to sleep. The memory of the break-in wasn't exactly restful, but although she tried to think of something else, she couldn't get the image of the black-clad man out of her mind. In the name of heightened security, she'd locked her bedroom door and stacked milk crates in front of it. It wasn't much, but it was the best she could do.

. . .

No one on *The Becky Belden Show* questioned the fact that Isabelle had been out sick the day before. She looked so awful—having gotten less than two hours of sleep, punctuated by nasty dreams—her story about a stomach bug seemed perfectly plausible. Clearly feeling sorry for her, the powers-that-be had assigned her light duty, organizing ingredients for the upcoming episode of *Food 'n' Friends* and sprucing up the guests' dressing rooms.

"Ah, there you are, Isabelle," said a voice behind her. "Leslie tells me you're a tad under the weather. I've brought you a little something to pep you up."

Isabelle stopped what she was doing—polishing a wide expanse of lighted mirror—and turned around to see Becky Belden herself standing in front of her, holding a blue ceramic tray covered with a linen doily.

Becky was dressed for the show, in an immaculate pink pantsuit, and the image was so perfect it might have come straight from the cover of her own magazine. Isabelle, for her part, had sweat under her arms and hair in her eyes. She also had her mouth hanging open at the sight of Becky Belden, *the* Becky Belden, waiting on her like a guest at Shelby's Landing.

"Er . . ." Isabelle tripped over her tongue, which had gone all rubbery. "Um . . . thank you, Ms. Belden. That's so kind of you . . ."

Becky Belden put the tray on the dressing table and touched hands to hips in mock indignation. "Now, didn't I tell you before that it's against the law to call me that? It's *Becky*, dear. Even the First Lady of our great nation calls me Becky. Have I made myself understood?"

Her smile, a thousand watts of charm, made it clear the lecture was all in fun. She came over to Isabelle and put a hand to her forehead, murmuring something about how pale she looked. "I do hope you're getting enough sleep, dear," she said, holding Isabelle's chin as she inspected her. On an episode of *At Home with Becky*, Isabelle had seen her use the same technique on the horses in her private stable. "Are you sure you're all right? You shouldn't be home in bed?"

"No, it's okay. I'm fine."

Becky shook her head, as though Isabelle were an errant

child. "You have to take better care of yourself, Isabelle. Remember, always be your own private nurse." It was one of Becky's many aphorisms. Isabelle still wasn't sure what it meant. "Now, I don't mean to be a Nosy Nellie," she said with a knowing smile, "but I have a feeling there's something else going on besides a little tummy trouble. Am I right?"

Isabelle wasn't sure what to do. Should she tell her about the attack? Becky's motherly manner made her want to confide in her, but Isabelle's late-night suspicions about the spate of deaths at BBM kept her silent.

At the same time, though, Isabelle felt ridiculous. The police themselves thought it'd just been another break-in, didn't they? And as for the other deaths . . . was she seriously thinking that there was some sort of evil conspiracy to kill BBM's employees? And that Becky—America's beloved queen of hospitality and good manners—was actually in on it? How crazy was *that*?

"It's all right, dear," Becky was saying. "You can express yourself freely here. BBM is one big happy family. If you're having problems at work, just go right ahead and share them with me."

"Uh, no, it's not that," she stammered. "It's just . . . I've got a lot going on. Personally, I mean."

Becky smiled and patted her on the shoulder. "Such as?"

"Oh, you know. Guy trouble. That sort of thing."

Becky made a clucking sound under her breath. "Not that nasty fellow whom you were engaged to marry. Not that awful"—it took her less than a second to come up with the name—"Laurence, I hope. He hasn't come around again?"

"Not exactly."

"Well, I should hope not. And I should hope that if he does, you'll tell him to go pound sand, as my mother used to say."

Isabelle nodded, too vehemently for her cranial well-being. Her hangover was still very much in evidence. "Definitely," she said.

"I'm extremely relieved to hear it," Becky said. Then she brushed Isabelle's flyaway hair back from her face. "Now, what you need is a nice aromatherapy sleep mask. I'll have Pat send one over for you. We grow the rosemary and lavender at Shelby's Landing. And I designed the pattern myself, as I'm sure you know."

"I, um . . . No, I didn't. Thank you very much." Isabelle swallowed, wondering what had become of her ability to speak English. Being in the presence of the great Becky Belden was making her light-headed. "And . . . I want to thank you again for giving me a job here. I really appreciate it. You really did me a huge favor."

Becky's smile became angelic, like something from Renaissance art. "Oh, it's *you* who are doing *us* the favor," she said. "When I read about you in the papers, I just knew you'd be perfect for BBM. And just look how well you're doing!" She gestured around the dressing room, as though Isabelle's mirror-polishing were worthy of a Daytime Emmy. "Now, I want you to have every bite and sip of this," she said, sliding the tray toward Isabelle. "It's some chamomile tea with tupelo honey and a nice peasant roll with *fraises des bois* preserves and unsalted butter. All from Shelby's Landing, of course. It's just the thing for you."

"Thank you, Becky," Isabelle said, resisting a starstruck urge to hug her. "This is really so nice of you."

"Oh, it's nothing," Becky said with a toss of golden hair. "I can't have my staff getting run-down on me, can I? Now, drink up. We have a very important show to do this week, and we need everyone to be at their best for it." She leaned in toward Isabelle, eyes glowing as though she were already under the stage lights. "In fact, if we're lucky and we work very hard, this episode just might save someone's life."

chapter 21

The Show was "Missing Persons: America's Secret Shame." Becky had subtitled it "My Very Personal Story," because the focus of the show was one of her own employees: Kenny Chesbro, the tech services worker who'd vanished two months earlier. The idea was to use his case to illustrate the epidemic of missing persons across the U.S. His entire family was going to appear on the show; Isabelle, who'd been out sick during the production meeting, had to scramble to memorize their names.

About two hours before showtime, Brynna came sprinting down the hall looking for her. "Have you seen Kenny Chesbro's sharing tape?"

"His what?"

"You know, the tape he made for Becky's Empowerment Archive. It's a DVD, actually. Have you seen it? It was in the control room this morning, but now nobody can put their hands on it."

Isabelle shrugged. "I've never even been in the control room. I'm not allowed."

"Oh, hell. Listen, we gotta replace it before Becky finds out and has a meltdown. She's gonna play it on the show—Kenny in his own words, that kind of crap. You gotta go up to the Friendship Center and get them to dupe another disc for you. Got it?"

Afraid to annoy her by asking just where the Friendship Center was, Isabelle went upstairs and found it herself. It proved to be a plush enclave on the thirty-first floor, with a half dozen upholstered chaise longues facing their own TV screens. In one corner were the inevitable coffee and pastries; in the other was an empty desk. A sign on it said:

We're Working Hard Helping People Share Their Important Individual Experiences, but If You Need Help We'd Love to Assist You! Please Ring the Bell and We'll Be Out in a Jiffy!

She rang the bell. Within an interval that Isabelle decided would, indeed, qualify as a jiffy, a young man emerged. She told him who she was and what she needed, and he said he'd have it for her in ten minutes.

Seduced by the lure of baked goods, she got herself a coffee and a frosted orange scone and settled in one of the overstuffed chairs to wait. Perched on one arm was a remote control; on the other was a laminated sheet with directions for using Becky's Empowerment Archive.

Isabelle eyed the remote. She'd never had the guts to check out her dismal performance that day at Shelby's Landing.

She punched a few buttons and discovered that her interview was even worse than she thought. She watched half of it—two minutes of herself blathering like an idiot—then decided she'd rather see someone else make a fool of himself. She called up Trevor's DVD in search of consolation. Unfortunately, he was such a ham he came off rather well.

On to the next.

Although she had her doubts that someone at Mac's level would have to participate in something so dopey, she took a chance and looked him up. And there he was, resembling a male model who'd been dragged to the dentist's office.

Whom else should she look up? She thought of Lisa, but she wasn't sure if the archive would still have tapes of former employees. But there she was, waxing poetic about her little rat dog; maybe once you went into the BEA—like the Roach Motel—you never got out.

Isabelle watched a few more tapes, and although the archive was supposed to be all about individuality, she thought there was a depressing sameness to the operation. Everybody talked about the little things in life that gave them joy, and although she knew she was being uncharitable, it all struck her as pretty lame. Lisa went on about her stupid pool, Trevor about his mannequin photography project, Mac about his penchant for sailing. Poor departed Marcia, reanimated by technology, spoke with shining brown eyes about the joys of sitting on her fire escape and watching the world go by. Loretta, neglecting to mention her status as a Mafia mom, talked about how she and her friends liked to have parties where they put together elaborate scrapbooks marking important events in their lives.

I wonder, Isabelle thought, if she has one titled "My Three Sons Go to the Joint."

.   .   .

The show began, as usual, with Mac Collins warming up the crowd. Isabelle could see him on the monitor in the greenroom, where she was babysitting Chesbro's relatives and the three other guests: an FBI agent, the head of a nonprofit group for friends and relatives of missing persons, and Jeffrey Bing, BBM's vice president for human resources.

The last time Isabelle had seen the latter, he was announcing the facts of Lisa's death to a gaggle of stunned employees. Today, as before, he was the calmest person in the room. His tie was done in the most perfect Windsor knot Isabelle had ever seen, and poking out of his jacket pocket was a matching silk hankie. He had his back to the monitor during Mac's opening act as though he couldn't care less; the only thing that seemed to interest him was the lamentable lack of Pellegrino in the greenroom.

Bing's composure only served to make the missing man's family seem more unhinged. Paul Chesbro won the award for Most Edgy; Isabelle watched him self-medicate with two entire bowls of cocktail peanuts. His wife—whose name was actually Paulina—kept crying and having to get her makeup redone. Their three daughters looked like they'd been chemically sedated.

Isabelle delivered them into the loving arms of an assistant producer, then stayed to watch from the wings. She'd only recently been given dispensation to be backstage during the show; Brynna had said, only half jokingly, that it meant she'd been promoted from peon to slug.

The cameras were turned off as the guests took their seats and the technicians tested their microphones. Meanwhile the makeup artist did yet another touch-up on Chesbro's mom, and Brynna triple-checked that Becky had four small, unopened bottles of Evian, her regulation supply.

Isabelle saw him out of the corner of her eye—Mac Collins, passing not ten feet away from her on his way to the greenroom. He must have seen her, but he didn't so much as wave. What was going on with him? She didn't have time to think about it because the swell of the theme music signaled the beginning of the show.

The episode opened with a photo of Kenny in a tuxedo; when the camera pulled back, it showed the rest of the Chesbro clan, all smiles at his sister's wedding. Then Becky started to speak, twisting the knife in the audience's collective gut.

"You're seeing one of the happiest days in the life of the Chesbro family," she said, slowly and with much drama. "This typical, hardworking American family lives outside of Green Bay, Wisconsin. Paul Chesbro is a master electrician. His wife, Paulina, owns a gift shop, selling local crafts and homemade fudge.

"On the day this photo was taken, the Chesbros were celebrating the marriage of their daughter Kayla. But today this family is grieving. Like nearly one hundred thousand American families, one of their own has gone missing. Exactly two months ago today, their son Kenny vanished without a trace."

The camera panned in on Becky. Even from a distance, Isabelle could see there was a tear in her eye.

"Now, Kenny's disappearance isn't just a tragedy for the Chesbro family. Kenny also belongs to another family, the family at Becky Belden Multimedia. For more than a year, Kenny Chesbro worked in BBM's technical services department, helping us make sure that our computers are in tip-top shape. Kenny was good at his job. Everyone he worked with just adored him. And now that he's gone, they miss him terribly.

"For the next hour, we want to share Kenny's story with you through the eyes of the people who love him the most. Now, throughout the show, you're going to see an 800 number on the screen. That's the number we need you to call if you have any information, any information at all, about the whereabouts of Kenny Chesbro. You don't have to identify yourself, and all the law enforcement agencies involved in the search for Kenny will keep the information strictly confidential.

"Now, we here at *The Becky Belden Show* know how much our viewers want to help people. We know you'll do this out of the goodness of your hearts. But we also want you to know that whoever provides information leading to the safe return of Kenny Chesbro will be eligible for a substantial reward. The Chesbro family has already offered twenty-five thousand dollars. Today Becky Belden Multimedia is matching that, for a total of fifty thousand dollars."

The crowd went wild. The Chesbros, who obviously hadn't been informed in advance, burst into tears en masse. Kenny's mother started mouthing "thank you, thank you" into a handkerchief. Becky went over to her, said something about how every mother in the audience must understand the pain she was suffering, and asked her if she wanted to share anything with the viewing public.

The woman made a visible effort to get ahold of herself. Then, twisting her hankie into a rope, she told the audience how much she missed her son. "He only called us once or twice a week," she said. "I used to think that wasn't very much. But now"—she started to tear up again—"now I'd give anything to hear the sound of his voice, just one more time." Becky put an arm around her. "And I just want to say . . . if anyone knows anything about what's happened to Kenny, please, just call.

And Kenny, if you can hear me . . . we all love you so much, and we just want you to come home."

She lost it. Becky, clearly sensing that Mrs. Chesbro was in no shape for any further sound bites, turned her attention to her husband. He echoed his wife's sentiments, though he mostly spoke to his lap.

"And I'd really like to give a big thank-you to the Becky Belden people," he said. "Those people have been real decent to us. Ever since Kenny went missing, they've been right by our side, night and day. Ms. Belden here, she even sent a lady over so my wife wouldn't have to do the housework. I . . . I can't imagine any company treating us better." He nodded, jaw clenched tight as though to stave off more tears. "You're a real special lady."

The audience leaped to its feet and applauded like mad. Isabelle started clapping, too; the atmosphere was intoxicating.

She was in midclap when she remembered she had to start setting up for the post-show reception, when Becky offered the audience coffee and brownies and basked in their adoration. She whirled around—and sprinted straight into the starched white cotton of a man's dress shirt.

isabelle let out a shriek that, to her horror, she later found out could be heard on the set. She clapped a hand over her mouth and stared up into a man's face—*way* up, because even though Isabelle was five foot eight, he had to be at least six-four.

"Oh my *God*," she said in an agitated whisper. "I'm so sorry."

The man looked down at her, seeming more bewildered than angry. Isabelle, for her part, was mortified. But she was about to become even more so; as she backed away, she realized she'd dumped the dregs of her coffee cup on the front of his shirt.

"Oh my God," she said again. She stood there, mouth ajar, as he inspected his shirtfront with the dazed incomprehension of a movie cop who'd taken one in the chest. She pawed lamely at the stain, but he waved her off.

"Don't bother," he whispered, returning his attention to the set. But the segment was wrapping up, the P.A.'s swooping down with water and tissues as they tried to keep the guests in a state of suspended animation until the show resumed; it wouldn't do if a grieving mother who'd been bawling before the commercial was all smiles after the break.

"Please let me help you wash that off," Isabelle said. The man looked at her like he was surprised she was still there. "There's some seltzer in the greenroom . . ."

"I think it's beyond that," he said. "Don't worry about it."

His voice was familiar; his face was, too. Where had she met him? His preppy manner reminded her of Mac, but she didn't think she'd ever seen them together.

The site visit with the Japanese publishers—that was it. He'd been the nice guy, the one who hadn't yelled at her when Lisa was AWOL. But what was his name?

"Please," she asked, "can I at least get you something to drink?"

Isabelle thought he was going to say no, but then he seemed to take pity on her.

"Black coffee," he said. "In a cup, not on my shirt."

She got him the coffee, managing to keep from dousing him with it. On her way back from delivering it, she ran into Brynna. Isabelle told her about her misadventure, describing the man and his low-key reaction to having coffee spilled on what appeared to be a very expensive shirt.

"Boy," Brynna said with a whistle, "you don't do things halfway."

"Meaning?"

"That's Bill Friedrich, the director of corporate communications. Otherwise known as one of the big cheeses of BBM."

.   .   .

Isabelle's desire to go home and hide was frustrated by Trevor—Trevor, her only real friend in New York; Trevor, who had rushed over to her apartment at two in the morning to keep her company when she needed him; Trevor, whose widowed mother was in town from Omaha and who desperately wanted Isabelle to, quote, "run interference" for him.

So Isabelle put on a demure skirt and baby-blue sweater set, which she deemed the right costume for her role as Trevor's adoring girlfriend. He was taking them to Tavern on the Green, a restaurant he could ill afford but which would keep up the fiction that he was making it in the dog-eat-dog world of window dressing. Isabelle had already promised to order the cheapest thing on the menu, and no appetizer or dessert.

Mrs. Hopkins was a generously sized woman dressed in what previous generations called their Sunday best. She wore an ankle-length blue skirt with pink roses, a matching blouse, and a hat wide enough to have its own weather system. Her perfume smelled intensely of lilacs; her lipstick was a shade not found in nature; her hair was big.

"So," Mrs. Hopkins said, "you're the Isabelle that my Trevvie's told me so much about."

Isabelle turned to her ersatz date. The use of the word "Trevvie" hung in the air between them.

"That's me," she said.

"It must've been awful to be jilted at the altar like that," Mrs. Hopkins said, patting Isabelle on the arm. "You poor thing." Isabelle kicked Trevor under the table as hard as she could. "Now, I hope you'll help me with Trevvie. I've been after him for years to get off his duff and get out there." She gave her son a disapproving look. "But does he listen to his mother?"

"Come off it, Mom," Trevor said. "Do you have to start on that again?"

She turned her attention back to Isabelle. "Do you speak to *your* parents like that?"

"I'm afraid they're both deceased."

Mrs. Hopkins' frown deepened, though Isabelle had a strange feeling she was enjoying herself. "Poor thing," she said. "Jilted *and* an orphan."

Trevor looked like he wanted to crawl under the table. "Mom . . ."

His mother dismissed him with a wave. "I tell him to march," she said. "I tell him to get out there and make some changes, make the world a better place. At least circulate petitions—something, *anything*."

Trevor put his head in his hands. "Jeez, Mom, couldn't you even wait until they bring the entree?"

"But does he listen to his mother? No, he just wants to go out and have a good time, or else stay home and play with his dolls."

"They're *mannequins*," Trevor said. "I told you a million times, they're—"

His mother slapped the table, so hard her iced tea gave a little jump. "How are we going to legalize gay marriage in our lifetime? How are we going to put an end to discrimination?" She dug into her voluminous handbag, pulled out a pamphlet, and waved it at Isabelle. "Do you belong to P-FLAG?"

"Um . . . no."

"But you should. It's Parents and Friends of Lesbians and Gays. I helped found our local chapter in Omaha. It's a really wonderful organization. We work to—" Isabelle tried to stifle a laugh; Mrs. Hopkins scowled at her like a disobeyed schoolmarm. "Have I said something funny?"

Isabelle took a gulp from her water glass and tried to stop cackling. "No, I, uh . . . I thought . . . When Trevor asked me to dinner, I figured he wanted me to pretend to be his date."

Trevor buried his head in his hands. "As *if.* I was hoping if you were here, maybe she'd lay off the guilt trip for once."

His mother made a clucking sound and patted Trevor on the back of the head. It seemed to be an affectionate gesture, but Isabelle noticed she was whacking him hard enough to agitate his dangly earring.

"Now, as I was saying," Mrs. Hopkins continued, "P-FLAG is a wonderful group. We work to . . ."

Mrs. Hopkins' discourse went on right up until dessert, which Isabelle decided she'd more than earned. Not that she didn't get a kick out of Trevor's mother; a fanatical gay-rights activist was definitely preferable to a fanatical homophobe. Isabelle just found the woman exhausting. Trevor, for his part, seemed ready to keel over.

His mother was scheduled to stay for three days. Sure enough, almost seventy-two hours to the minute after she'd arrived, Isabelle got an e-mail from Trevor asking her to join him for a drink to celebrate her departure.

He and his posse, as he called it, were convening at exactly the kind of bar Isabelle hated: a big, loud, crowded dance club that was a meat market for single people of all sexual persuasions. And what was worse, the place used to be a *church*; although Isabelle's Jewish father and Catholic mother hadn't raised her in any particular faith, she was still horrified at the concept of drinking a Cosmo where the altar used to be.

Figuring her debt to Trevor would be paid in full, she donned a miniskirt and tank top and went downtown. It took her twenty minutes to find him among the undulating throngs;

he was bellied up to one of the club's three bars, surrounded by a dozen people Isabelle knew only vaguely. A couple of them had been there the night she'd gotten trashed on green-apple martinis and spilled her guts about her sordid love life; the others were Trevor's friends from the mail room and elsewhere around BBM.

Isabelle elbowed her way to Trevor's side, figuring she could make an appearance for half an hour and get the hell out of there. There were already a clutch of martini glasses littering the bar, most of them with just a sip or two of something left. Clearly, the party was in full swing.

Trevor greeted her with a sloppy hug and a sloppier kiss; he smelled of gin.

"What in God's name are you drinking?" She pointed at his glass, which looked like it contained something from the Slurpee machine at the 7-Eleven.

"It's a BMW," he said, shouting to be heard over the noise. "Stands for Blue Moon in Winter. Gin and blue curaçao over crushed ice. It's the latest thing. Want one?"

"Hell no."

"Then what can I get you?"

"I'll have a vodka martini."

"Shaken, not stirred?"

"Whatever."

He ordered a round of martinis for the group, but she'd barely had a sip before she was dragged out onto the dance floor. She protested that she couldn't possibly dance without at least "one entire drink" first, but he wouldn't take no for an answer. She dutifully shook her booty for the remainder of the Madonna remix, then escaped while Trevor and his friends were still shaking theirs with considerable enthusiasm. She collapsed on the bar stool and asked the bartender for a glass of water with no ice, which she drank in one long gulp.

"You're *hot*," said a voice behind her. "You're a *hottie*."

She looked up to see a man standing over her, clad in black leather pants and a short-sleeved shirt with a red dragon painted on it. He had very curly black hair, muscular arms, and a facial expression that bespoke extreme intoxication.

"I was watching you out on the dance floor. You sure can *move*. So . . . what's your name?"

Isabelle stared at him, wondering when Trevor and his twelve closest friends were coming back. The man was hovering over her; she feared the slightest loss of balance would send him careening onto her lap.

"Come on, gorgeous," he said. "What's your name?"

"Um . . . Isabelle."

"*Isabelle*," he howled. "A beautiful name for a bee-yoo-tee-full girl."

"Thanks." She swiveled away from him and faced the bar.

"Hey, come on, you don't have to give a guy the cold shoulder. Bring those gorgeous titties back around here so I can see 'em."

She stayed exactly as she was. From the corner of her eye, she saw a trio of similarly clad men watching approvingly; his buddies had apparently sent her drunken Romeo on a mission.

"And those *legs*," he went on. "I gotta tell ya, you got the kinda legs a guy wants to have wrapped around his ass. So whadaya say? How about you come back to my place for a little horizontal—"

His monologue was interrupted by the splash of a drink in his face.

The guy rubbed his eyes as though he couldn't quite figure out what had happened. His friends exploded into a chorus of chuckles; he himself blinked at Isabelle with a distraught expression, as though she'd just broken his heart. Then, to Isabelle's great surprise, he wandered away without another word.

"Well, I see I can't take you anywhere civilized."

It was Trevor, who'd been observing the action from a safe distance.

Isabelle dried her hands with a cocktail napkin. "Thanks for coming to my rescue."

He plucked a martini off the bar, took a sip, and chased it with a melodramatic sigh. "Izzy, my love, when will you learn to play nice with the other kiddies?"

"When they stop telling me they like my titties."

"I see. Shall we repair to the apse?"

She spent the next hour sitting on a red velvet divan, drinking a fresh cocktail and making small talk. When she decided she'd put in her time, she tried to say good-bye to Trevor, but he was nowhere in sight.

"Where'd Trevor disappear to?" she asked one of the still-indistinguishable members of his posse. "I haven't seen him in a while."

"Little boys' room."

"He's been gone a long time."

The man's lips formed a sly grin. "Maybe he made a new friend."

She stood up. "Well, tell him I said good night."

"Go tell him yourself. The litter box is coed."

Since she was in need of a little nose-powdering, Isabelle decided to swing past the bathroom on her way out. She didn't see Trevor amid the crowd, which included four people making out and two others buying drugs. It was just as well: she was in no mood to catch him with his zipper down.

She'd just finished using a frighteningly unhygienic toilet when she recognized her neighbor: one of Trevor's red and white bowling shoes was poking out from under the partition between the stalls.

"Hey, Trevor," she said, knocking on the thin metal wall. "It's Isabelle."

No response.

"Oh, *Trev*-ee," she said in a singsong voice, "are you in there?"

Still no answer.

"You okay over there?" She knocked again. "Hey, how drunk *are* you? Jesus, did you pass out or something?"

She nudged his foot with hers. It didn't move.

chapter 33

isabelle was starting to get worried.

She went around to the door of Trevor's stall and peeked through the gap between the partition and the door. She saw him sitting on the john, fully clothed, slumped against the wall. She knocked on the door again, calling his name and asking if he was okay. When he still didn't answer, she forced the flimsy door open with a light touch of shoulder against metal.

She rushed to Trevor's side and shook him. His head lolled against his chest, eyes closed. A trickle of vomit ran down his chin. She felt for a pulse, but she couldn't tell for sure if he had one.

Isabelle felt the side of his face: it was warm. She slapped his cheek, told him to stop screwing around and wake up, but he didn't.

She ran out of the stall and shouted at the necking couple to call 911. One of them must've gone out and told the management, because within seconds a beefy man in jeans and a tight black T-shirt came in and told everyone to clear out of the bathroom. Isabelle ignored him, crouching on the dirty floor while the man pulled one of Trevor's eyelids back and felt the side of his neck.

"Son of a bitch," he said. "Another goddamn OD." He shook his head, clearly furious at Trevor for screwing up his evening. Then he turned his anger on Isabelle. "What the fuck was he on? Did he cop it in here?"

"What? I don't know. For chrissake, help him."

"He's dead, you stupid bitch." The bouncer grabbed Isabelle's little black purse off her shoulder and dumped the contents on the bathroom floor. He scattered her things—lipstick, house keys, ID—as he pawed through them. "Where is it? Is it in his pockets? You goddamn well better flush it before the cops get here. I am *not* getting shut down again because some stupid dickwad doesn't know how to get high. So come on, we don't have time to fuck around. What was he on?"

"I don't know," she said, tears starting to choke her. "I don't think he was on anything."

He dismissed her with a shake of the head and started going through Trevor's pants pockets. He pulled out his wallet, keys, and the roll of licorice candies Trevor had been using to keep his mother from smelling cigarettes on his breath. Finally, she had enough.

"Get away from him," Isabelle said as the man dug into Trevor's shirt pockets. "Get away from him," she repeated, grabbing at the back of his shirt. "I swear, if you don't, I'm telling the cops."

That seemed to do the trick. He stopped what he was doing and turned on Isabelle, his face a mask of disgust. "You people are pathetic," he said. But he let go of Trevor's shirt, violently enough to make the body fall off the john and onto the floor.

He left Isabelle like that, her friend lying on the dingy tile as she scrambled around on her knees, desperately trying to find her house keys before the police arrived.

.   .   .

Trevor was dead. And New York's finest didn't seem to give a damn.

Overdoses at the club were nothing new, and it seemed that the opinion of the officers who arrived at the scene was that Trevor was a victim of his own stupidity.

Once the police and EMS arrived, Isabelle was evicted from the bathroom and told to wait in the manager's office. It was over an hour until a detective came to speak to her, writing down her contact information before proceeding to grill her about Trevor's drug habit. She told him that she'd never known him to do anything stronger than pot, which the cop seemed to believe not at all.

It was after eleven by the time he let her go. In a flash of decency, he offered to have a uniformed officer drive her back to her apartment, and on the ride uptown, she asked whether someone was going to notify Trevor's mother. The cop took down her name and where she lived, and said the department would do it as a matter of form. That, at least, was a relief; the prospect of having to tell Mrs. Hopkins had been haunting her since the moment she got up from the bathroom floor.

She didn't actually burst into tears until she was in her apartment. Just getting past the doorman had taken all the strength she had left, and when she got inside, she leaned against the closed door and slid to the floor. She sobbed so hard it left her throat raw and sore, her tears drenching the hem of her skirt as she clutched her knees to her chest. Finally, when she couldn't cry anymore, she wandered around the apartment with no idea what to do. Habit took her into the bedroom, where she left her clothes in a pile in the corner and crawled under the sheets.

After ten minutes in the dark, she reached for the phone. It rang only once.

"Dr. Leonard-Brill."

Her sister sounded rushed, vaguely annoyed. Isabelle nearly hung up, but the awful emptiness of the apartment made her hesitate.

"Dr. Leonard-Brill here. Hello."

"Hi, Margie? It's Isabelle."

An exasperated pause. "How many times have I told you to call me Marguerite?"

"Sorry, I . . ." She felt the tears start to rise up again. "Listen, have you got a minute?"

"Not really. I've got surgery in the morning, and the twins are—"

"I'm sorry, it's just . . . I really need someone to talk to. A friend of mine just died. Tonight."

"I'm so sorry," her sister said in a tone she probably used with teenage girls who didn't like the results of their nose jobs. "What happened? Are you okay?"

"Yeah, I . . . I'm just kind of all alone here, you know?"

"Tell me what happened."

"We were at this club, and I think he overdosed. The police wouldn't tell me anything."

Isabelle could hear her sister's quick intake of breath from the other side of the continent. "Overdosed? The police? Good Lord, Isabelle, who in the world are you associating with?"

"I . . . He's a friend from work."

"A friend from work who goes to clubs and takes drugs and gets himself killed? What kind of friend is that?"

Normally, her sister's condescending tone would have made her angry. But she felt so awful, so sad and vulnerable and alone, that all she could do was cry. "You didn't know him," she sobbed into the phone. "He was the sweetest guy you ever met."

"Listen to me, Isabelle," Marguerite said, now sounding like she was talking to one of her six-year-olds. "I'm sorry your friend is dead, but I really think you need to take a hard look at the choices you're making."

"The choices I'm—"

"Come on, Isabelle. I'm not going to baby you. Ever since you graduated from college, your life has been a mess. First you can't even figure out if you want to go to graduate school, then your marriage falls apart before it even starts. And now you're hanging around with some sort of degenerate who—"

Isabelle hung up the phone.

She lay on the bed, feeling as alone as she ever had in her life. The emptiness was like an ache, and when she started to cry again, she felt like a baby wailing over some physical discomfort it couldn't put into words.

She couldn't believe that Trevor was dead, couldn't believe that she wouldn't see him the next day, blabbering about some new indie band he wanted to see. Neither could she believe that she really had no one in the world—that if she opened her bedroom window wide and threw herself out of it, no one would shed a tear.

She couldn't stand it. She was desperate for human companionship, for someone to tell her she mattered.

Without letting herself think about what she was doing, she put her clothes back on and went downstairs. She stood on Lexington Avenue with her arm raised, and the taxi came so fast it felt like the universe was aiding and abetting her. She gave the address, a place she'd never been before. She paid the fare and walked into the lobby, her mind still fixated on one thing, like an old LP that was stuck on a skip.

There was no one at the front desk, and therefore no need to explain herself to a stranger. She took the elevator to the eleventh floor and found apartment F. She rang the doorbell.

When there was no answer, she rang it again.

he must've been in bed—not asleep, but reading or watching TV. He was wearing a pair of gym shorts, which Isabelle suspected he'd just pulled on. On his left side, the waistband of his boxers was peeking out over the top.

"What are you doing here?" he asked.

His tone wasn't unfriendly. It wasn't even all that surprised. Maybe having lonely women show up on his doorstep in the middle of the night wasn't particularly unusual.

She stood in front of him. It occurred to her that now would be a good time to have second thoughts about what she was doing, but she didn't.

"Could I come in?"

"Of course," he said.

He closed the door behind her. She'd always wondered what Mac's apartment would look like, but now the surroundings barely registered—glass coffee table, leather couch, widescreen TV.

"Can I get you something?" he asked. She shook her head. "Are you all right?" She shook her head again.

She stepped to the living room window and stared at the Empire State Building, lit up in purple and gold for some obscure holiday.

"I'm all by myself," she said. She stared out the window some more. "I hate it."

He took a step toward her, then stopped. "We're friends, aren't we?"

"I never had a clue what we were."

"I'm sorry about that. But I told you, I—"

"I didn't come here to talk about it."

She crossed the distance between them, took his face in her hands, and kissed him. There was none of the reserve she'd practiced before; she pressed her body against his, as though she could shed her isolation by passing it on to him like the flu. Being with him—not just anyone, she realized, but *him*—seemed as necessary as breathable air. She wasn't sure why, and she wasn't sure if she'd feel the same way in the morning, but at the moment, she didn't care.

She felt him hesitate, resist—even in her present state, she knew this wasn't the healthiest way to jump into bed with someone. She felt for the hem of his T-shirt and snuck her hands underneath it, running her palms up along the muscles of his back. It must've had the desired effect, because she felt something in him cut loose. He kissed her, more aggressively than he ever had before, and when he slid his hands down to her waist and pulled her toward him, Isabelle knew that they weren't going to stop short of the bedroom. Something fluttered in the pit of her stomach; it felt like victory.

They stood there clenched like that for a while; how long, she couldn't imagine. She kept expecting him to carry her to the bed, but after a while, he pulled away from her and put out a hand. She was confused at first, but eventually, she figured it out. He was asking her to make something resembling a rational choice.

She couldn't bring herself to look him straight in the eye, but she put her hand in his. He led her to the bedroom, a matter of only a few steps; Mac Collins made a lot of money, but this was still a Manhattan apartment.

There was a reading light on by the bed, and the sheets were tousled. She'd been right about what he'd been doing when she showed up on his doorstep. He kissed her again, their bodies pressed together. Isabelle hadn't worn a bra to the club, and she wasn't wearing one now. Their upper bodies were separated only by the thin material of his T-shirt and her tank top, which felt less like an impediment than a tease.

Eventually, even that seemed like too much. He slipped the thin black straps off her shoulders, let them hang there for a while, then pulled them down so the top was bunched at her waist. She responded by pulling the shirt over his head, and the sensation of their naked chests against each other was electric. She ran her hands along his upper arms, something she'd been itching to do since the first time she saw him in a T-shirt. His hands were busy along her spine, at the nape of her neck and the curve of her backside. In one swift movement, he yanked her clothes to the floor—tank top, miniskirt, thong.

"Jesus Christ, Isabelle," he said. "You're beautiful."

That was when he finally lifted her onto the bed. His sheets still felt warm from when he'd lain there a few minutes earlier. She pulled him down toward her and wrapped her legs around him, tugging at the waistband of his shorts. She couldn't get them off—their bodies were too much entwined—and after she'd flailed around for a while, he laughed and shed them himself.

. . .

Oblivion. That's what Isabelle had been after, and that's what she got. For the better part of an hour, she didn't think about anything. Not about Trevor, or her sister, or the mess that had become her life—or whether leaping into bed with Mac Collins was a good idea.

Eventually, though, the real world had to intrude; they had to deal with each other from the neck up. It happened about six-thirty in the morning, when the sun reflecting off the building next door hit Isabelle in the face, and she woke to find herself lying naked next to Mac.

It probably didn't bode well for her emotional maturity that her first instinct was to flee. She tried to lift his hand off her gently, so as to avoid waking him, and as she pried each finger in succession, she felt like a player in some idiotic sex comedy.

When she finally got free, she shimmied over to the edge of the bed and rolled off. Scuttling about on her hands and knees, she hunted for her clothes. Her tank top she found soon enough, but her miniskirt and underpants were missing in action.

"What are you doing down there?"

She froze, tank top half on, her lower half exposed.

"For chrissake, stop skulking around on the floor and come back to bed."

Not seeing much of an alternative, she stood up and squirmed her way back to where she'd been lying. In the name of modesty, she'd grabbed a corner of the bedsheet to cover her nether regions.

"Don't you think we're a little past that?"

There was a mocking tone in his voice that Isabelle didn't like. But then again, she had been trying to sneak out without saying good-bye. What would her former girlfriends in Burlington have said about a guy who did that?

She lay next to him in the bed, not sure what to do or say. She felt like a heel for trying to flee, but as she inspected the halogen light fixture on the ceiling, she understood the instinct: this kind of awkward silence was just what she'd been trying to avoid. Finally, to her great relief, he put an arm around her and snuggled her in toward him. After a moment, he posed a question to the top of her head.

"Why did you come over here last night?"

She didn't say anything at first. She was worried the answer might not be flattering to either one of them. Finally, she just said, "I didn't want to be alone."

"Ah." He sounded disappointed, and Isabelle thought he probably had a right to be.

"Wait." She rolled over so her chin was on his chest. "It's not the way it sounds. I didn't want to be with just anybody. I wanted to be with you." He nodded, not very convincingly. "Look, I don't do this a lot. Maybe in college, but not for a long time. And not at all since Laurence."

"What happened last night?"

She told him what had happened at the club, how she'd found Trevor unconscious in the bathroom, how the bouncer had been so hateful to her. She told him about calling her sister and getting the usual lecture about her own shortcomings. He seemed to understand that the evening's events had sent her to his doorstep, but whether it bothered him she couldn't tell.

"Do they have any idea what he took?" Mac asked.

Isabelle shook her head. "I told you, the strongest thing I ever saw him do was pot. I guess he drank a lot, though. And the truth is, he definitely wanted to cut loose. Having his mother visit kind of sent him around the bend."

"I'm sorry," he said, shaking his head. "I'm really sorry you had to be there."

"Me too. I guess I really didn't know him. We'd only met my first day at BBM, and that was only around a month ago." She pushed her hair back over her head. "Jesus, his poor mother. Her husband's dead, and Trevor was her only kid."

"What a mess," Mac said. The alarm went off then, and he vaulted out of bed. Isabelle tried not to stare. "I've got to get to the office," he said. "And you probably need to go home and change."

"Yeah."

"I'm gonna grab a shower."

"Okay."

He took a step toward the bathroom, then turned back. "If you wanted," he said, "you could join me."

she found out the cause of Trevor's death while she was standing in the Cosmopolitan Diner, one hand on the counter and the other on a pot of decaf. Someone had left a copy of the *Times* open to a page with metro news briefs, and the headline caught her eye: CLUB DEATH BLAMED ON DATE-RAPE DRUG.

Isabelle knew she'd had a sheltered upbringing in northern Vermont—small town, no violent crime, teenagers who considered mailbox baseball to be a major form of rebellion. But even she knew what "roofies" were.

The technical name was Rohypnol. Isabelle had known a girl at the University of Vermont who'd had it slipped into her drink at an off-campus party, and woken up twelve hours later. She was lying in a pile of leaves, naked, and the police told her there was evidence she'd had sex with three different men. She didn't remember a thing.

But although Isabelle had heard of roofies, she didn't know that the drug wasn't just used for date rape. People also took it in combination with other drugs, to extend a high or soften a low. She also didn't know that it could be fatal. And according to the NYPD, there was enough in Trevor's bloodstream to kill someone twice his size.

The paragraph from which Isabelle absorbed this information was barely two inches long—hardly enough to make her feel like she'd been kicked in the gut. She blinked back tears as she waited on her two lone tables, neither of which had ordered enough food to generate more than two dollars in tips.

"Miss," beckoned one of her customers, a beleaguered mother of two who looked like she could use a slug of something strong in her coffee. "Would you mind getting us another water?"

Isabelle looked down at the three glasses, which were full. "Is there something wrong?"

"She drank out of mine," said the woman's son, a little boy of about five. Isabelle stared at him, not understanding. The boy aimed a finger at his sister. "She's got cooties," he explained, as though that said it all.

"I do not," said the girl.

"Do so," said her brother.

The children were close enough in age to be twins. Isabelle, feeling for the woman, got another water. She also got herself a couple of Advil.

She was clearing their table an hour later, wondering if she'd ever be cut out for motherhood, when something occurred to her.

Something awful, something that made her feel both terrified and guilty.

Mrs. Mendes noticed—the woman never missed anything—and when she asked Isabelle if she was sick, all she could do was nod that she was. Her boss said she should go home, and Isabelle didn't argue. She walked out onto the street still wearing her uniform and apron, her order pad still in the pocket, her purse hanging from the shoulder where Mrs. Mendes had placed it.

She didn't go home. She dug a business card out of her wallet, one the police detective had handed her as she was leaving the club the night Trevor died. It had all been so perfunctory—*if you think of anything else, give us a call*—and it was obvious that he never expected to hear from her. In fact, he seemed to think that the whole proceeding was way beneath him; Isabelle got the feeling that the only reason he'd been dragged into it was the club's reputation as a cesspool of sin.

The detective's name was Jay Ellis. But when she went to the address on the card and asked for him at the precinct's front desk, she was told he was on vacation. Could another detective help her? Fine, she said.

She waited for twenty minutes, until a white man in his mid-fifties came down to see her. She'd expected to be taken upstairs, but he seemed content to talk in the lobby.

The first thing she noticed was that he had powdered sugar on his tie. The second was that there was a tan line where his wedding ring used to be.

Isabelle wasn't sure why these things struck her, but they did; if she'd been the detective, she would've guessed that the man's wife had just evicted him and he was eating doughnuts three meals a day.

"So what can I do for you, Miss . . ."

"Isabelle Leonard. I'm here about the death of Trevor Hopkins." She watched the detective try to retrieve the name from his mental Rolodex. He couldn't do it. "He died at Club Catechism on Tuesday night. I was there. That other detective said I should call if I thought of anything."

The man finally seemed to know what she was talking about. "That latest OD. Right. Case's pretty much closed."

"But I read in the paper that the thing that . . . What he died of was Rohypnol. Roofies. And—"

He shrugged. "Kids today'll take pretty much anything."

"But that's just it. I don't think he took it. I think somebody poisoned him."

The detective's hair was mostly gray, though he had a full head of it. He ran his hand through one side as Isabelle spoke, a gesture that struck her as dismissive. "Now, why would you say that exactly?"

"Because—"

The front door opened, and two uniformed cops dragged a young man inside. His hands were cuffed behind his back, and his dyed-red hair had been shaved into a Mohawk. He didn't go easy, but the detective barely seemed to notice. Isabelle flattened herself against the wall until they'd passed by, the prisoner howling like a monkey in the jungle.

"Listen," she said, "about a week before Trevor died, a man broke into my apartment. He threw a radio at me while I was in the bathtub and tried to kill me. And then the other night at the club, I tossed a drink in some guy's face. I figured it was mine, but maybe it was Trevor's. Maybe he drank mine by accident and the roofies were in it and they were supposed to be for me."

The cop looked at her like she was speaking in tongues. "Look, lady, I know you're real upset about your friend and all. But what you're saying sounds pretty far-fetched."

"But—"

"You called in the B and E?"

"Of course, I did."

He crossed his arms. "And what did the cops think?"

There was a hefty dose of sarcasm in the question. Isabelle tried to keep a grip on her temper.

"They said it was just another burglary, okay? Jesus, could you even *pretend* to take me seriously?"

He rubbed his eyes, hoping it might make her disappear. "I've got a lot of cases to clear," he said. "I don't have time for hysterical females."

"*What?*"

"What do you want me to say? That I think your junkie boyfriend didn't really OD himself trying to chase his high? No, what really happened was some criminal mastermind went into a crowded bar, in front of God and everybody, and spiked your drink as part of his big plot to kill you." He didn't try to hide his smirk. "Yeah," he said, "that's a lot more likely."

She was still fuming by the time she got home. It didn't help her mood to realize that she was still wearing the hideous waitress uniform, which felt as bad as it looked.

She thought things couldn't get any worse. Until she checked her answering machine and realized that she'd been mistaken.

chapter 26

"hello . . . isabelle?"

The voice sounded empty, exhausted, elderly beyond her years.

"This is Dorothy Hopkins. Maybe you remember me from"—the woman paused, trying to catch her breath—"from dinner with Trevvie last week. I'm sorry to bother you, but I was hoping . . . I know this may be an imposition on you, but I don't know who else to turn to. I should do it myself, I'm sure, but"—another long breath—"I just can't bear to go back there. I do hope you understand. Thank you very much."

The machine clicked. Isabelle was standing there, wondering what to do with the incoherent message, when the machine beeped. The second call was also from Trevor's mother.

"Dear me," she said. "I'm afraid I didn't say what I called for. I'm so mixed up . . . But the reason I called is that I was hoping you'd be kind enough to take charge of Trevvie's things for me. The personal things, photographs and letters, I'd like to have. The rest . . ." She spoke slowly, and Isabelle got the feeling she was reading from a list, like she'd written it down so she didn't forget again. "The rest, feel free to give away to whoever needs it. Perhaps some of his friends might like his clothing and his records, that sort of thing. If there's any money, I'd appreciate it if you'd donate it to ACT UP. That's the AIDS Coalition to Unleash Power. I'm sure you could find the number in the telephone book. Thank you very much."

She hung up. There was one message left on the machine. Isabelle had a bad feeling she knew who it was.

"Isabelle, dear, it's Dorothy Hopkins again. Trevor's mother? I'm calling to apologize for asking you to take care of Trevor's things so soon after . . ." It was a cheap answering machine, but it captured the sound of her crying. "I wouldn't ask it of you, but I have to have his apartment cleaned out in less than a week. I hope you understand. If you have any questions, don't hesitate to call."

She left her phone number. Isabelle could barely make it out through the sobs.

.   .   .

Isabelle could've done it alone if she had to, but she was glad she didn't. Help came in the form of Mac Collins, who showed up at the diner as though it were a usual Saturday—and not, as it happened, the first time they'd seen each other since their late-night interlude in his bedroom.

And their early-morning one in his shower.

He hadn't been expecting to spend the afternoon cleaning out an overcrowded studio in Alphabet City, but if he minded, he didn't let on. She collected the clothes in trash bags, packed the photos and letters into manila envelopes, clustered the mannequins in one corner. The place didn't have to be vacated for a few days, and she figured she'd ask some of Trevor's mail room friends to spread the word that his stuff was up for grabs. The stereo she kept for herself, along with Trevor's collection of CDs. The only other thing she would've taken for sentimental reasons—his beloved red bowling shoes—happened to be the ones he'd died in. God only knew where they were, and after what she'd seen at the club, she hardly wanted them.

"Mac," she said as they surveyed the one-room apartment, dingy walls now exposed by the absence of movie posters. "If I tell you something, do you promise you won't just say I'm crazy?"

"Don't tempt me."

"I'm not kidding."

"Okay. What is it?"

Fueled by her grief, she told him what had happened—the attack in her apartment, how she and Trevor might have swapped drinks just before he died, her fears that she might have been the real target. She stopped short of telling him her concern about the mortality rate among BBM employees, partly because she was afraid he would laugh at her.

But there was another reason. She still couldn't quite shake the memory of that night in the storeroom, when she thought that one of the men removing boxes might've been Mac. The man, whoever he was, had the same vocal tone, even used a few of the same expressions. She'd barely known Mac then, so she wasn't anywhere close to sure. The fact that both Mac and the mystery man wore Bruno Magli wing tips, which had seemed so striking when she was huddled behind the boxes, had faded in importance when Isabelle noticed a dozen more pairs in the elevator.

In short, Isabelle didn't know what to think. But at least at the moment, she couldn't deny the fact that although she was now sleeping with Mac Collins, she still didn't entirely trust him.

"So . . . what did the police say?"

"I told you," she said. "This detective called me a hysterical female."

"You get his name?"

"No. Why?"

"So you can make a complaint."

"That's not what I'm worried about right now. What do you think about what I said?"

"You mean, do I really think there's someone out to get you? You haven't made any mortal enemies since you moved to Manhattan, have you?" He smiled, trying to make light of it. It wasn't the reaction she was looking for.

"Jesus, you're not taking me any more seriously than the cops did," she said.

"Look, I'm sorry. I just find it hard to believe that your friend Trevor's death wasn't exactly what it appeared to be. What happened in your apartment is something else again."

"What do you mean?"

"I mean, if somebody wanted to rob the place, why go into the bathroom? And throwing your radio in the tub? What the hell is *that*?"

"That's what I thought. The cops said it was just a thief who was looking for whatever he could lay his hands on, and when he saw me, he panicked."

"I suppose they know their business," he said. "But it still sounds fishy to me."

She kissed him on the cheek. "Thank you."

"For what?"

"For agreeing with me." She saw a dark look pass across his face. "What's wrong?"

"I just thought of something," he said. "Do you think this could have anything to do with all that attention you got?"

"You mean 'Give 'Em Hell, Isabelle'?" She bit her bottom lip. "God, I don't know. I never thought about that. You mean, like, a stalker or something?"

"I guess so."

"I don't know," she said. "It's not like I've been getting crank calls or anything. What kind of stalker just decides to cut to the chase and try to kill you?"

"I have no idea," he said. "It was just a thought. Maybe not a very smart one."

They hauled the stereo uptown to her apartment via taxi, and Mac hooked it up for her. Just when she thought he was going to spirit her into the bedroom, he kissed her good-bye and said he had to spend the evening at the office.

Left to fend for herself for dinner, she concocted a couple of English-muffin pizzas—spaghetti sauce from a jar, shredded mozzarella, a few slices of pepperoni, the chopped-up bits of a desiccated green pepper.

She ate the pizzas sitting on the floor with a can of Diet Coke while she perused Trevor's CDs. Most of the albums were by bands she'd never heard of, but the collection seemed to be eclectic—some jazz, heavy metal, new wave, a lot of dance remixes. She found a copy of the sound track to *Willy Wonka and the Chocolate Factory*, which seemed out of place until she discovered that the case contained not a compact disc but a half dozen neatly rolled joints.

"Trevor," she said with a wistful smile, "you little rascal."

She debated for a minute, then lit up one of them and took a deep drag; she told herself it was in honor of Trevor, but it had more to do with her own anxiety. Trevor's stash turned out to be strong stuff, and she felt it almost immediately. The next thing she knew, she'd returned to the kitchen to make a few more English-muffin pizzas, which she somehow toasted without burning down the apartment.

She was still pawing through the CDs, thinking that she'd be having a lot more fun if Trevor were there with her, when one of the cases caught her eye.

It had a logo on the front, a bright red square with a black lobster in the middle. She knew she'd seen it before, but she wasn't sure where. She didn't think Trevor had ever played the album for her—come to think of it, she didn't think she'd seen the logo on a CD at all.

So . . . where?

if she were in her right mind, she probably wouldn't have fixated on it. But in her present state, Isabelle was determined to figure out where she'd seen that lobster logo before. She started flipping through her photo albums, but within minutes she abandoned them; memories of life back in Vermont were killing her buzz.

She moved on to some magazines she'd filched from the recycling bin downstairs, but she still didn't find it. The idea of looking at magazines made her feel like she was on the right track, though; she crammed another muffin-half into her mouth and wandered around the apartment.

In the corner of her bedroom was a stack of copies of *Becky* she'd brought home from the office. She opened the most recent one, flipped through the pages, and there it was: the photo of Kenny Chesbro that had been blown up and put under glass in the BBM lobby. He was wearing a ripped T-shirt, and on the front was a red square with a lobster in the middle. It was a perfect match.

HAVE YOU SEEN OUR FRIEND?

That's what the headline said. A whole six pages had been devoted to his disappearance, not to mention an entire hour of *The Becky Belden Show*. Obviously, the company was doing its utmost to find Kenny Chesbro—yet another example of Becky's largesse.

It's the Chesbro thing for sure.

That's what one of the men in the storeroom had said as they loaded boxes onto a cart. Then he'd said something about it being a wild card, that it might bite them on the ass.

What had he been talking about? How did "the Chesbro thing" have anything to do with taking boxes out of storage? Isabelle couldn't remember any of the labels, but she was pretty sure they'd all been people's names—she remembered thinking they were probably personal property, like the box of stuff that had belonged to Marcia Landon. Trevor's casual attitude about what she'd seen that night had convinced her it was really nothing. But now, after all that had happened, she had the feeling her instincts had been right in the first place: something weird was going on.

It's the Chesbro thing for sure.

Why did Kenny Chesbro's disappearance prompt the late-night raid on the storage room? She tried to recall the names on the boxes, even just one, but she couldn't. All she could come up with were questions. Was Kenny still alive, or was he yet another BBM employee who'd met an untimely death? And were those other deaths really something extraordinary?

Isabelle tried to remember who they all were, but she wasn't thinking coherently enough to keep them straight. She grabbed a pencil and notepad and wrote down everyone she could think of.

Marcia Landon—pushed in front of subway train
Lisa Kinne—drowned in swimming pool
Doreen Fusco—hit by car
Trevor's friend—meningitis (he went to funeral)
Pinkie—OD'd on something
P.R. guy—allergic reaction to something (I signed sympathy
  card)
Trevor Hopkins—OD'd on roofies
Kenny Chesbro—vanished

Eight people, at least seven of whom were dead. And of those seven, six of them had died in totally unrelated ways; the only exceptions were Trevor and Pinkie, the "wastoid" girl he'd mentioned from the mail room, who'd both overdosed on drugs.

She needed to find out more about them. But how?

She eyed the new laptop, which she still hadn't returned to the store despite her dead grandmother's hectoring voice telling her it was the ethical thing to do. The computer had come with a free trial membership to an Internet service; Isabelle plugged in her phone line, signed up, and did a Web search for "Doreen Fusco."

Doreen was the one Loretta had told her about, the woman from circulation who'd been hit by a car. A number of stories came up, including a piece on the accident—a hit-and-run on Northern Boulevard in Queens, which was apparently a notorious death trap.

Isabelle also found a couple of obituaries, one of which had a photo. Doreen Fusco was a friendly-looking woman of sixty-one, who'd spent her adult life caring for her elderly parents, now dead; her only sibling, a brother, had predeceased her.

She'd never married, had no kids, and was a pillar of Our Lady of Mount Carmel Catholic Church, which was now in the market for a new organist.

Next, she looked up Marcia Landon and found the stories about her death on the track of the L train at the 14th Street station, and her killer's subsequent confession and incarceration in a mental hospital. She found one obituary, from a paper in Marcia's rural Pennsylvania hometown. It noted that she'd been a member of the Spirit Squad in high school and had earned a degree in communications at Penn State. She had no siblings, and her parents had died in a car accident when she was in college.

Marcia had no immediate family. Neither did Doreen. Was *that* a common denominator? But Trevor's mother was still alive, and Isabelle had met Kenny Chesbro's heartbroken relatives in person as well. It had to be something else.

Or was she just really, really stoned?

Leaving the detritus of her pizza orgy on the floor, she took another look at the CD that had set her off. The band was called Klaw; the music, once she put it on the stereo, was a folky roots-rock that Isabelle found a tad whiny. When she got to a ballad about the importance of recycling, she turned it off.

She looked up Klaw on the Web and found a home page that appeared to have been designed by an eight-year-old. It had a tour schedule, some grainy photos of fans camped out in tents, and a P.O. box where you could send fifteen dollars in exchange for a self-produced album. As far as she could tell, there was nothing special about the group; there were a thousand others just like them, playing in minuscule clubs as they waited for their big break.

Isabelle scratched at her scalp, which had suddenly come over all itchy. Her mouth was superdry, like her tongue had been suctioned at the dentist's. She got herself a big glass of water, unplugged the computer from the Internet, and brought both back to her futon. In the short interval between the laptop's arrival and Trevor's death, she'd taken a stab at reconstructing *Princess Astra and the Attack of the Fire Robots*, but she hadn't been able to piece it together. She'd started fooling around with an as-yet-untitled romance, but she thought her heroine was a simpering dolt—not an ideal formula for a best seller. No, she needed to move on to something else.

True crime.

The words leaped at her—not off her bookshelf, but from somewhere in her pot-addled brain. Wasn't that a genre that always sold like hotcakes? She sat up, sure she could almost see the dollar signs floating in front of her face.

What if there really was something going on at BBM—something sordid and deadly—and she was the one who wrote a book about it? What if some nut job was somehow picking off BBM employees for sport, and she told the story—the *inside* story? Wouldn't that sell books by the bucketload? Maybe Hollywood would even buy the movie rights . . .

Her brain was invaded by the image of her favorite college English teacher, the one who'd taught her *Ulysses* and *Persuasion* and *Richard III*. What would he say about Isabelle's choice of commerce over art?

To hell with him, she thought; he's got tenure, anyway.

But what if there was really nothing going on—what if the seven deaths were unrelated and there was some harmless explanation for Chesbro's disappearance? After all, even though

Marcia thought she was being stalked, her actual killer had confessed; didn't that close the door on her story at least?

Well . . . even if there was no true-crime story to tell, maybe she could turn it into a thriller, a real page-turner. One thing was for sure: there were enough characters at BBM to fill a dozen novels.

All she had to do was figure out what the hell was going on. And write it.

.   .   .

It had seemed such a good idea when she was half in the bag. A few hours later, as Isabelle walked down Lexington Avenue, writing the book on BBM seemed more problematic.

How was she supposed to find out what was happening— she, who had no experience whatsoever in police work, private detection, or even journalism? True, she did watch a lot of cop dramas, but that hardly seemed to qualify her; from what she'd seen of the NYPD, art didn't exactly imitate life.

She sighed, tightening her raincoat against the light summer shower. It wasn't much of a night for a walk, but she needed some fresh air; her apartment smelled like an Arlo Guthrie concert. She wasn't sure why she'd been stupid enough to smoke one of Trevor's joints. At least, she thought as she walked, her last act before leaving the apartment had been to flush the rest of them down the toilet.

Isabelle liked New York in the rain. The gloom tended to match her mood, and it kept people off the sidewalks. She was also partial to the way all the city lights were reflected in the puddles and how the enterprising guys hawking their cheapo umbrellas seemed to appear from out of nowhere.

She walked nearly twenty blocks down Lex, almost a mile, and when she saw an all-night diner, she figured she could afford a cup of coffee. She wound up splurging on a slice of blueberry pie with whipped cream, and as she sat there reading someone's discarded *Daily News*, she wondered how much longer she'd be living in the city. Once she had enough money to move, where would she go?

Later, she couldn't say that she'd really noticed the man who sat in a booth at the far end of the restaurant; she was too absorbed in her own angst about the future. She barely registered the fact that he kept looking at her, and if she did notice it, she would've thought it was just because she was a disheveled mess. She paid her bill, left a generous tip in honor of the waitressing sisterhood, and walked back out into the rain.

It was only later, as she made her way back to the apartment she could barely afford, that she realized someone was following her.

she'd barely registered the man's presence in the diner, and when he'd walked out just seconds after she did, it didn't seem out of the ordinary. Still, Isabelle was new enough to the city that she always felt a bit on edge; she made it a habit to look behind her on the streets, especially at night.

The man, dressed in black pants and a brown leather jacket, was a block behind her. At the corner of 79th and Lex, she'd stepped into a bodega to buy a quart of milk and a jar of peanut butter. When she came out, he was still there—still a block behind her, chatting on a cell phone.

There was nothing disturbing about that, not in a city of eight million people. But when she paused to look at some leather boots in a shopwindow, he stopped as well. She walked faster, suddenly getting scared. But a few blocks later, when she dared to sneak a look over her shoulder, he was nowhere in sight.

She felt incredibly relieved; she'd concocted the entire thing in her true-crime-obsessed brain.

She stopped to catch her breath outside another bodega, whose sidewalk was a riot of color from the racks of flowers for sale. She'd always been tempted to buy them—they were actually quite affordable compared to the prices back home—but she'd never dared to spend the money. It didn't cost anything to smell them, though, so she stepped inside the clear-plastic curtain that had been put up to protect the flowers from the rain. She pulled out a bunch of violet-colored roses and gave them a long sniff. When she exhaled, it was a sigh of relief.

Then she looked up and saw him again. His image was distorted through the rain-dappled plastic, but she was sure it was him—leather jacket, black trousers, baseball cap.

Where had she seen him before? What was it about his build, the way he walked, that rang a bell?

The answer came to her in a flash. The man who was following her had been a customer at the Cosmo Diner—the young blond guy who tipped well, who hadn't minded when she accidentally brought him French toast instead of pancakes.

He was also the man who'd broken into her apartment. She knew it instinctively from the way he moved—that smooth, feline stride. It was him; she wasn't sure why she was so certain, but she was.

She retreated inside the store. Had he seen her looking at him? She didn't think so; he'd been glancing in the other direction.

What should she do?

She shrank back farther into the market. It was steamy inside, the heat and moisture generated by the hot-food bar kept in by the plastic curtain. She stood next to the counter, a narrow space overloaded with candy bars and muffins and plastic-wrapped half-moon cookies.

"You wanna buy?" The Korean man behind the counter indicated the roses. Isabelle had forgotten she was holding them. She hesitated, feeling utterly paralyzed. "Five dollar," he said. It came out *fi-dollah*. Isabelle reached into her pocket and pulled out a ten-dollar bill. He gave her change and wrapped the flowers; she watched him put a plastic bag around the dripping stems and a sheet of paper around the bouquet, wishing he wouldn't work so fast so she'd have more time to think.

She walked out slowly, pausing inside the plastic to see if she could locate the man. She couldn't, but she had a feeling he was still there.

She kept walking up Lexington, a chilly sweat forming in her armpits; she felt as if she knew what it was like to be a prey animal, as though she'd suddenly slipped a few links in the food chain.

What should she do? She asked herself the question again, but she still had no answer. She thought about turning onto a side street, but the crosstown blocks were long and much more dimly lit. She decided to stay on Lex.

She crossed to the west side of the street, where a half dozen people were gathered at a bus stop; surely, there was safety in numbers. When the M101 came, it occurred to her that even though it was going in the opposite direction from her apartment, it might be a good idea to get on.

The bus was crowded, and she couldn't get a seat. She stood in the aisle, trying to catch a glimpse out of the rain-speckled windows. Two blocks south of where she'd gotten on, she thought she saw him standing on the corner.

She was right. He was in line for the bus.

She tried not to panic, tried to work her way to the back door without drawing attention to herself, but she was having a hard time. The rain had lured people onto the bus who otherwise would've walked, and her route to the exit was blocked. A native New Yorker could've gotten out the back while the passengers were coming in the front, but Isabelle couldn't manage it.

She was three-quarters of the way down the aisle when she saw him. He slid his MetroCard into the slot to pay the fare, then started working his way toward her. For a half second, their eyes locked.

His expression was calm, almost pleasant. It was a look Isabelle never expected, and she found it utterly terrifying.

She kept fighting her way toward the back door, and when the bus came to the next stop, she was poised to leap off. She hailed the first cab she saw and was about to give the driver her home address when she thought better of it. She had him take her to Trevor's—thank God she still had the key with her. When the cab dropped her off, she sprinted up the five floors and triple-locked the door behind her.

Only later, as she was trying in vain to sleep on the bare Murphy bed amid Trevor's mannequins and rolled-up posters, did the irony strike her. She'd always been terrified of his neighborhood, but at the moment, she was much more terrified of hers.

. . .

The cost of a new, allegedly unpickable lock on her apartment door drained her TV fund down to zero. But she had no choice. Trevor's place had to be vacated in a matter of days, and anyway, it wasn't as though she could hide out there. She had to go to work, and anyone who wanted to follow her could just pick up her trail from there.

She could run, as they say, but she couldn't hide.

Running had been very much on her mind over the past day. In the middle of her first and only night in Trevor's coffin-sized apartment, she'd seriously debated the idea of taking off. Surely, somebody in Burlington would let her crash, especially if she offered to do all the housework. And failing that, she could always put her tail between her legs and beg her sister to take her in for a while. But first she'd have to ask her to send her the money for a bus ticket to L.A.; then she'd have to sit through endless lectures and tiptoe around Margie's palatial house like the poor relation that she was. The more she thought about it, the less it appealed.

And there was another thing, a feeling that asserted itself around four in the morning.

The truth was, she was sick to death of running. She'd run away from her small town to Burlington, she'd run from herself when she agreed to marry Laurence, and she'd been running from the memories ever since he'd ditched her at the altar. She was afraid if she kept running, she might never stop— might never figure out who she really was, what she really wanted.

Did she want to stay in New York or leave? Find a better job or go back to school? Keep seeing Mac Collins or not?

But it wasn't just a desperate need for renewed self-respect that was keeping her in the city. There was also the simple truth that, after all she'd been through over the past few months, she needed to know what the hell was going on. Why was someone after her? What was really happening to the people at BBM? Had Trevor's death been an overdose or murder?

Isabelle knew she was taking a risk, maybe a big one; she was headstrong, but she wasn't crazy. She was well aware that a saner person would probably have ignored all the questions and just gotten out of Dodge—would have cut ties, pulled up stakes, and vanished.

Vanished, she thought. *Just like Kenny Chesbro.*

chapter 29

The thought struck her as crazy, structurally unsound, but she took it for a spin, anyway.

Could it possibly be true—that Kenny Chesbro wasn't dead, he was *hiding*? But why? His family hadn't been able to come up with any reason why he'd disappear; but then again, out-of-town relatives were hardly the best source of information about what a twenty-something guy was up to in New York City.

Could it have anything to do with what was going on at BBM, whatever it was? And if he really *was* hiding, was there any way for Isabelle to find him—when the police, private detectives, and his own family hadn't been able to? She'd seen Kenny's whole life dissected on *The Becky Belden Show*, and she still had no idea where to start.

After work on Tuesday, Isabelle left the TV studio and went up to the Friendship Center. Her mission: to dig up information on the deceased BBM employees on her list.

Pinkie, Trevor's acquaintance from the mail room, was a girl named Debbie Luft. Her nickname, she'd learned by asking around the employee lounge, was inspired by her hair, which was dyed the color of cotton candy. On the sharing tape, she came off even worse than Isabelle had; she was shifty and abrupt, answering questions with little more than a grunt. When she was asked about hobbies, all she said was that in the not-too-distant past she had done a lot of heroin.

She also mentioned that her parents were dead, she didn't have any family, and she wasn't dating anyone.

The same was true of the man for whom Isabelle had signed a sympathy card on her first day of work in special projects. His name, she'd learned from her friend Loretta, was Alan Setzer; he'd worked in the P.R. department, which struck Isabelle as an unlikely place for a fellow who seemed shy to the point of agony. Just watching his video, Isabelle felt instantly sorry for him—and not just because he was dead. Setzer had lost his whole family in a house fire when he was a teenager, and he seemed incredibly lonely. At one point, he introduced the camera to his "best friend": the EpiPen drug injector he carried because of a severe allergy to peanuts. Apparently, his good buddy had let him down; Isabelle recalled that he'd died of an allergic reaction.

Next, she looked up Doreen Fusco. The woman seemed sweet, if a bit careworn. She said she was proud to be a native of Queens, that she lived in the same house her grandmother had come to as a bride; she also said she'd just joined Jenny Craig with a goal of losing fifty pounds, and she was walking around the neighborhood for exercise.

Isabelle hadn't been able to track down the name of Trevor's friend, the one who'd died of meningitis. For lack of any other ideas, she punched up Lisa's video again. There she was, wearing too much makeup, babbling about the glories of her little rat dog and that stupid rooftop swimming pool.

Holy Christ.

Isabelle's fingers trembled as she pushed the buttons on the remote control to call up Marcia Landon's video. She fast-forwarded until she got to the end, to the part where Marcia had talked about how much she liked to sit on her fire escape.

Marcia's boyfriend had said she was afraid someone was trying to kill her. And it all started when the railing of her fire escape collapsed, and she nearly fell to her death.

Marcia talked about the fire escape, and she almost fell off it.

Lisa talked about the pool, and she drowned in it.

Pinkie talked about her heroin habit, and she died of an overdose.

Alan Setzer talked about his peanut allergy, and he died of an allergic reaction.

Doreen Fusco talked about taking walks around Queens, and she was run over by a car.

Isabelle talked about taking baths and listening to the radio, and someone tried to electrocute her in the tub.

The thought made Isabelle gasp. She looked around the Friendship Center to see if anyone had heard her, but she was alone.

Was this the link she'd been looking for? Of the seven people who'd died, at least five had mentioned particular facts about themselves that subsequently played a role in their deaths. What's more, all five of them had no immediate family. And as far as anyone knew from her tape, neither did Isabelle; in the interview, to avoid talking about her sister, she'd said that she was an only child.

Suddenly, the Friendship Center didn't seem so friendly. She dropped the remote on the armrest of the overstuffed chair, and it slid off and fell to the floor. She stood up, overcome with a desire to get the hell out of the Belden Building.

She knew it made no sense, but she was instantly afraid that her insight was a two-way street—that just as the common denominator among the victims had become clear to her, whoever was behind it could see that she knew. It was illogical, melodramatic, asinine; but then again, she was almost positive that she'd just been followed by the same man who'd tried to murder her.

I'm not paranoid, she thought. *It's just that everyone's out to get me.*

She left the Friendship Center and walked down the hall, forcing herself not to run. There were still a few employees in the hallways—it was only a little after six—but Isabelle's anxiety made her feel as though they were all staring at her, contemplating the best way to make her death look like an accident.

She walked out of the building and up the Avenue of the Americas. It was rush hour in Midtown, and there were more people on the street than in Isabelle's entire hometown. For once, the crowd was a relief; instead of suffocating her, it protected her. She found a coffee shop on a side street, an old-fashioned place that reminded her of the Cosmo, and she took a seat in the corner—back to the wall, so no one could sneak up on her. She ordered a Diet Coke; she was too agitated to eat.

In her mind, she went over the list again: Marcia, Lisa, Doreen, Pinkie, Alan, Trevor, Kenny . . . Isabelle. The ninth, Trevor's friend, she hardly knew anything about—just that he had worked in the building, was gay, and had died of viral meningitis. She took a long sip of her drink and decided to put him aside for the moment.

One of these things is not like the others.

As a child, she'd always loved that game. When her family took long car trips, her parents would give her and Margie workbooks filled with those sorts of puzzles. As she thought about the eight victims, it seemed to her that two of them weren't like the others: Trevor and Kenny. Both had families, for one thing. Trevor hadn't mentioned anything on his video-tape that hinted at the manner of his death—like Lisa and the pool or Alan Setzer and his peanut allergy—and Kenny might actually be alive.

So what if you took them out of the equation? What if, as she'd been thinking earlier, Kenny was really on the run? And what if Trevor hadn't been the intended recipient of the Rohyp-nol; what if the drug had been in the drink, and Isabelle had been the target?

It didn't make her feel good. But she thought it made sense.

She drained her soda and ordered another. She wasn't in the mood to be frugal.

Okay, she thought, let's assume that Kenny is out there somewhere. What could he be running from?

If it was something personal, something unrelated to what-ever was happening at BBM, then there was no point in worry-ing about him. It occurred to her that maybe he'd run because an attempt had been made on his life, but she doubted it; Kenny had family, which didn't fit the pattern. So what was it?

She pulled out the notebook in which she'd written every-thing she knew about Kenny. It had a pink satin cover, deco-rated with hearts and flowers; it'd been a bridal shower present, her "honeymoon journal." The fact that she was now using it to record the facts surrounding seven deaths struck her as appropriate.

Kenny was from Green Bay, Wisconsin. He'd shared an apartment in Brooklyn with three people, none of whom knew him well; he'd only moved in a few weeks before he disappeared. He'd worked in tech services, most recently trying to fix problems with the company's e-mail server. He didn't have a steady girlfriend, though his roommates had heard him bring girls home. He called his parents twice a week, on Sundays and Wednesdays, just like he'd promised his mom when he moved to New York.

She read through the next four pages of details about Kenny's life. It didn't seem like much.

She thought about going to talk to his roommates about him, but she couldn't see the point. The police and private detectives had already spoken to them, to no avail. Ditto for his coworkers.

She flipped through the pages again. What do I know that they don't?

Her eyes landed on a note about the band whose T-shirt Kenny had been wearing. Klaw, with the silly lobster logo. It was so obscure it had never occurred to Isabelle that it stood for anything; if she'd noticed it at all, she would've thought he'd just bought it on a trip to Maine or something.

Was it worth pursuing? At this point, she couldn't think of anything else. Why the hell not?

feeling a little calmer, Isabelle walked out onto the street in search of a record store. She remembered there was a big chain a few blocks north of the Belden Building; maybe she could find another CD by the same band. She entered the revolving door, got distracted, and revolved right out again. Maybe she was more agitated than she thought.

When she finally made her way inside, she went to the rock section and looked under "K." It wasn't there. She asked a clerk, who stopped chewing gum long enough to look up the band on the computer.

"They only got one album in the system, and we don't carry it," she said. She leaned closer to Isabelle, like she was afraid her boss might hear. "Ya might wanna try Vinyl Destination in the East Village. It's on St. Marks. They got all sorts of obscure shit."

Isabelle found the place an hour later, after taking the subway downtown and asking several scruffy-looking people for directions. The store was smaller than Trevor's apartment. It was decorated with posters for bands Isabelle had never heard of, as well as an assortment of signs detailing the penalties for shoplifting. The single employee was wearing a pair of camouflage combat pants, a black mesh tank top, and a ring through his nose.

He eyed her warily when she walked in, like she might ask if he had a copy of *The Best of Bread*. Isabelle knew she didn't look like she belonged there. When she asked if he knew anything about the band Klaw, he smiled so broadly it made his nose ring wiggle. She asked if they'd released more than one album; he said not yet, but he heard they were working on one.

"I was wondering," Isabelle said, shouting to be heard over the screech of the music blaring from the store's sound system, "do you know where you could pick up one of their T-shirts? The kind with the logo on the front?"

"They sell 'em on tour. That's about it. The Klaw Kids wear them like a uniform. You know, you write all the places you been on the back."

"Klaw Kids?"

He eyed her suspiciously. "I thought you were a fan."

Isabelle tried to sound nonchalant. "I'm interested in them, yeah. I'm trying to learn more about them."

That seemed to mollify him. "Well, then you gotta go to a show. That's what Klaw's all about—not that studio shit. And, you know, they let fans tape their shows and trade 'em, just like the Dead."

"So you mean they're kind of like the Dead and Phish? People follow them around?"

"Yeah. Some guys do nothing but. Just go place to place, maybe pick up some work here and there. It's like its own little world, man." He smiled, like he was talking about the joys of life in the Land of Oz. "No rat race and shit. Great way to drop out of your life for a while, see what really matters. You should check it out sometime."

"Er . . . maybe I will," she said. She tried to maintain normal breathing; an idea was forming in her head, and she was afraid to hope that it might be right. "Do you know how I could find out where they're playing next? I couldn't find much about them online."

He smiled, again sending the nose ring awiggle. "Klaw Kids aren't really into that shit. It's way too . . ." He couldn't seem to find the word he was looking for. He shrugged instead.

"So do you know how I could track them down?"

"It's all kind of word of mouth. I could ask a couple people and give you a buzz—if you wanna, like, leave me your digits."

The prospect of having her phone number seemed to give him way too much pleasure. Isabelle smiled, thanked him, and said she'd call him instead.

.   .   .

The next time Isabelle thought she saw the man who'd tried to kill her, she was in the cereal aisle at D'Agostino's supermarket.

She'd been debating the merits of Corn Chex versus raisin bran, both of which were on sale, when she heard a crash at the end of the aisle; a woman had bumped into a display, knocking over some boxes of Quaker instant oatmeal. Isabelle automatically turned around to look, and out of the corner of her eye she saw a man in a gray sweat jacket disappearing around the corner.

She didn't think much of it until she was in the produce aisle. She looked up from a pile of peaches to see a man staring at her from the other side of the store—a blond man in his twenties, wearing a gray sweat jacket, gym shorts, and a baseball cap. The man who'd been in the diner and the bus and her apartment.

He turned away as soon as she spotted him, heading down along the meat coolers at the back of the store. Isabelle stood there frozen, peach in hand. After a couple of seconds, she came to her senses, ditched her groceries, and headed for the exit. But he'd already beaten her there; she watched, utterly confused, as he went out the door and down the street.

It was as though she'd scared him off. But that didn't make any sense; he was the one who was stalking *her*. Not sure what to do, and feeling safer in the market than outside of it, she wandered back to where she'd left the basket full of groceries. She paid for them and walked out onto the street. She looked around for the man in the gray sweat jacket, but she couldn't see him. As she walked up the street, the shock she'd felt at the sight of him wore off and was replaced by real fear.

If he'd found her in the supermarket, he must've tailed her from work. She'd seen him following her once before—but how many times had he done it unseen? And what was he trying to accomplish? It wasn't as though he could make an attempt on her life in the middle of a crowded street.

Could he?

She had to go to the police. Even if they were as condescending as the detective on Trevor's case had been, she thought, they'd at least have to do *something*.

As it turned out, that something involved having Isabelle look at hundreds of pages of mug shots while drinking stale coffee, her frozen chicken pot pie melting in the corner. The cops in her home precinct had been more polite than the detective downtown—this was the Upper East Side, after all—but they hadn't been much more helpful. A detective listened to her story, nodded at all the appropriate moments, and observed that she seemed to be under a lot of stress. He wrote down the man's description and told her that if she ever saw him again, she should call 911 on her cell phone. When she said she didn't have one, he looked at her like she was an alien, and a rather pathetic one at that.

She scrutinized the mug shots for over an hour, until her eyes hurt and all the faces began to run together. It was awful to keep staring at the array of bad guys, this grainy yearbook immortalizing the twenty-something white guys of Criminal High. She wondered what terrible things they'd done, what people they'd hurt. How many of them were murderers, rapists, armed robbers? And how scary was it that they looked just like everybody else?

. . .

Isabelle didn't want to spend the night alone, but she didn't think it would be a great idea to show up on Mac's doorstep again. She asked one of the doormen to carry her groceries upstairs for her, just so she wouldn't have to enter her apartment by herself. As he was about to leave, she told him she was still nervous after the break-in and asked him to check the apartment to make sure no one was lying in wait for her. It seemed to appeal to his vanity, and he did it with gusto. There was no one there.

She locked the door after him and put the groceries away. The chicken pot pie didn't appeal, so she shoved it into the freezer. She ate one of the peaches, then settled in front of the snowy television with the six-pack of day-old cupcakes she'd picked up in the sale bin. They were decorated with roses and had an orange sticker on top that said $1.29. Plucking one of the chocolate ones from its plastic perch, Isabelle was well aware that she was self-medicating. She really didn't care.

With her noncupcake hand, she pulled a card from her purse and picked up the phone. The proprietor of Vinyl Destination sounded glad to hear from her—maybe a little too glad—but he didn't yet have an answer for her. He'd keep trying.

She was halfway through the cupcake package—two chocolate, one vanilla—when the phone rang. She grabbed it, assuming it was the guy from the record store. She was wrong.

"Hello?" she said.

"Isabelle." There was no question in his voice; he knew it was her.

"Who is this?"

"I think you know."

Isabelle felt her stomach twist. The cupcakes, so recently soothing, threatened to come back up on her.

"Who is this?" she asked again.

"I've never known anyone like you," he said.

"Who *is* this?"

"I'm very good at my job," he said. "You have no idea how good. Until you, I've had a perfect record. I've never failed."

"Why are you following me?" He didn't answer. "Why are you trying to kill me?"

There was a pause. Then he said, "That's what I do."

"Who are you? Why won't you leave me alone?"

"I can't," he said. Something in his voice made her believe him.

"Who are you?"

Another pause, longer this time.

"Are you enjoying the computer?"

"What?"

"The laptop I sent you to replace the one I took. It's much better than your old one. Don't you think?"

Isabelle had no idea what to say. She sat there, the phone held against her ear by a trembling hand, and waited for him to speak.

"You should use it to write something important," he said. "Not those foolish stories you were working on before. They're beneath you."

"What—" Isabelle's voice cracked. "What do you want from me?"

After another long silence, the man said, "I don't know."

he hung up the phone so quietly Isabelle barely heard the click. She was still sitting there ten minutes later, trying to make herself breathe in and out at something resembling a normal rate, when the intercom buzzed. The sound nearly made her jump out of her skin. On wobbly legs, she walked over and answered the doorman's summons.

There was someone to see her. He gave the name, and Isabelle gasped. After a few more deep breaths, she said to send him up.

It was Mac Collins, and he was holding a bouquet of flowers.

"I'm sorry to drop in on you, but—" He did a double take. "Are you okay?"

"I'm . . . not really sure."

"What's going on?"

"Do you want to come in?"

"I'm already in. What's the matter?"

"Do you want something to drink? Coffee or something?"

"For chrissake, Isabelle—"

"Let's just have a drink, okay? Is Knob Creek all right?"

He nodded. "Is that frosting on your face?"

She swiped at her cheek. "Would you, um, excuse me for a minute?"

She ran into the bathroom and checked herself in the mirror; there was indeed a swath of chocolate frosting on her left cheek. She rinsed it off and shoved the rest of the cupcakes in the bedroom closet. By the time she'd reappeared in the living room, Mac had poured drinks for both of them.

"I'll go put those daisies in water," she said.

"Already done. I couldn't find a vase, so I put them in a glass."

"Thanks." She only had one vase; it was in the bedroom, holding the roses she'd bought on the street the night she caught the blond man following her. They were wilting badly. "Um, do you want to sit down?"

"All right." They sat on the living room floor, backs against the wall.

"Did you stop by for any particular reason?"

"Maybe I just wanted to see you."

"Oh." Then, "Er . . . that's nice."

"But you want to know the truth? I've been working like crazy this week, and—"

"That's a shock."

"— and when I stopped for five minutes, I remembered you weren't a certain kind of woman."

"What are you talking about?"

"The kind I usually date." He shrugged against the wall. "You know, good times, no strings . . ."

"Oh."

"Since we . . . Since the other night, I haven't exactly been Mister Romance. I'm not really used to it, not in a long time, anyway. So I thought I ought to make an effort."

"Oh." She wasn't quite sure what to say. "So here you are. Making an effort."

"Yeah," he said. "So how about you tell me what's got you so upset? When I came in, you were white as a sheet."

"I . . . I just got an upsetting phone call."

"Bad news?"

"Sort of."

"You want to talk about it?"

"Not really."

"Is there anything I can do?"

She thought about it. "You could console me," she said.

. . .

The cupcakes reemerged an hour later, when they were lying on her futon and he mentioned he'd worked straight through dinner. He made some comment about having discovered the source of her frosting-face, and chose a vanilla one. He lay on the bed with the cupcake balanced on his chest, Isabelle not quite sure that she wasn't hallucinating; such things were normally confined to the realm of female fantasy.

Later, when she wondered why she'd decided to tell him everything, she knew it had a lot to do with this mood of easy intimacy. Mac was obviously trying to be a nice guy, and she had to admit she found it charming. Not just charming—disarming.

"Isabelle," he'd said as he lay beside her on the sheets, "are you sure you're okay?"

"How do you mean?"

"You seem like you've got a lot on your mind."

"Well, yeah. I sort of do."

"Do you want to talk about it?"

"I'm not sure."

"It might make you feel better. Don't you think?"

And then she'd told him everything; not only the fact that the man who'd broken into her apartment was still after her, but her fears about all the recent deaths at BBM. He listened, lying still and not saying a word. She told him about the recordings at the Friendship Center, how they seemed to offer handy tips to a potential murderer. The story took her a long time; she hadn't even gotten to the part about Kenny Chesbro's disappearance when he interrupted her.

"Don't go to work tomorrow," he said.

"What? I can't just—"

"Stay home. Just stay in your apartment and don't go anywhere. Okay?"

"But I—"

"Promise me." He was already putting on his pants.

"What are you doing?"

"I have to go," he said.

And he went. Afterward, she realized he never even said he was sorry he had to leave.

. . .

When her alarm went off in the morning, Isabelle had no idea what to do. Should she really stay home from work? If she did, what excuse could she give? And more to the point, why had Mac fled her apartment faster than he could zip up his trousers?

Kicking the empty cupcake package out of her path, she made her way to the bathroom and took a shower. Although she wasn't hungry, she made breakfast as a way of avoiding a decision. She was waiting for the teakettle to boil when the phone rang. She answered it, but warily.

"Hello?"

"Hey, Isabelle?"

The voice was unfamiliar. She was instantly on guard.

"Yes?"

"It's Zee from Vinyl Destination. How ya doin'?"

It took her a second to place him. "How did you get this number?"

"Caller ID."

"Oh." So much for her attempt at anonymity.

"I got some info for you. I tracked down my buddy, the one who's huge on Klaw. Turns out they're in Providence. Not in the city, in some town just outside—Pawtucket. Doing a gig at a club called the Bucket. The Pawtucket Bucket, get it? Tomorrow night they go down to Charlotte. Then, um, Bangor. Kind of ass-backwards, huh?"

"Thanks. I really appreciate it."

"So I was, like, wondering . . . Do you have a boyfriend or anything?"

She managed to get off the phone without either offending him or agreeing to go out with him. The kettle whistled, and she fixed a cup of tea and toasted a frozen bagel while she made a plan.

The phone call had made up her mind for her. Yes, she'd skip work, but she wasn't going to stay home. She'd been thinking about what the record store guy had said before—that following Klaw was a "great way to drop out of your life." If she was right that Chesbro was alive and on the run—admittedly, something of a wild guess—then what better place for him to hide? As far as she knew, no one but she had made the connection between him and the band; it hadn't even been mentioned on *The Becky Belden Show*, when his life had been dissected in excruciating detail.

What could make him so determined to hide that he wouldn't even contact his parents—would let them suffer for months as they wondered if he was alive or dead? Was that even possible? From what Isabelle had heard of Kenny, he didn't seem like a callous person. So did that mean that he really *was* dead? Or was his fear of being found that strong?

There was only one way for her to find out, and she had to move fast. The next day the band was heading for North Carolina, which was a lot farther away than Rhode Island.

She called *The Becky Belden Show*'s production office and left a voice mail for Leslie saying that her stomach bug had come back, trying to sound appropriately infirm. Then she grabbed her biggest purse, filled it with some toiletries and a change of underwear, and took the subway to Penn Station. The round-trip ticket on Amtrak cost over a hundred dollars, even if she avoided the express. She gritted her teeth and handed over her credit card.

The trip took three and a half hours. In Providence, she found her way to the bus station and waited half an hour for a bus to Pawtucket. While on board, she ate a king-size Snickers bar and wondered what the hell she was doing.

When she got off the bus, she went into a decrepit-looking package store and asked for directions to the club. The sixtyish woman behind the counter glared at her through narrowed eyes.

"You ain't one of *them*, are ya? Ya look too decent."

"One of who?"

"Them long-haired hippie creeps what've been hangin' around the past few days."

"Oh, no," she said. "What would make you think that?"

"'Cause they ain't got nothin' better to do 'n trail after that group what's playin' at the Bucket. Comin' in here askin' for grapefruit juice and somethin' called PowerBars. Do I look like I got that sort o' thing? Well, do I?"

Isabelle allowed that she didn't, then asked if the club was nearby.

"Round the corner and down the block," she said, as though Isabelle were intensely simple for not knowing. She was somewhat mollified, however, by Isabelle's purchase of a snack-sized bag of pork rinds and a bottle of Yoo-hoo; it seemed to indicate that Isabelle might be her sort of person, after all.

She carried the food with her to the club, too revved up to eat despite her hunger. Her arrival was anticlimactic; she found the place deserted. If there hadn't been a sign out front touting the headliners for tonight's show—KLAW WED THU FRI 8 PM—she would've thought the building was abandoned. The Bucket was a dilapidated roadhouse that couldn't have amounted to much even in its glory days; at the present moment, she was surprised the walls were still holding up the roof.

She knocked on the front door, but it was locked. She went around to the back, where an overflowing Dumpster had created an aromatic nightmare, and found the two other doors locked as well.

She was walking away, resigning herself to coming back for the eight o'clock show, when the front door opened. The man who emerged had a scraggly ponytail without much hair on top; he was holding a roll of duct tape big enough to fit around Isabelle's neck.

"Excuse me," she said. "I'm looking for Klaw."

He looked her up and down, taking in her tailored slacks and white cotton blouse. Both came from J. Crew. "Are you for real?"

"I'm really looking for their fans." She smiled at him, hoping it made her appear trustworthy. "Actually, I'm looking for my brother. He's been following them around, and we haven't been able to reach him. But I have to get in touch with him, because our grandma's in the hospital."

The lies, absurd as they were, came easily. But it didn't matter, because the man clearly didn't give a damn.

"Klaw Kids are staying over at the Dugout," he said. When she didn't appear to get it, he added, "Local rat hole doesn't care how many people you jam into a room, or how high you get when you're in it."

He gave her directions to the motel, which was about a mile away. She ate the pork rinds and drank the Yoo-hoo on the journey, feeling increasingly deflated. What did she think she was doing, spending money she didn't have to go on some wild-goose chase around the outer armpit of Rhode Island? By the time she got to the motel, she was more than ready to get back on the train to New York, where she planned to spend the rest of the day in bed berating herself for being such an impulsive moron.

The Dugout was as advertised—a regulation rat hole. It had once been light blue, but the shutter hinges had dripped a foul-looking brown rust along the facade. There were weeds sprouting through cracks in the parking lot, and two of the rooms were boarded up with sheets of plywood. Along one side were the remains of a pathetic little asphalt playground, now nothing but a few metal posts and a set of sagging monkey bars. In the far corner was a netless basketball hoop, under which a half dozen young men were playing a pickup game; a boom box was blasting the Grateful Dead at earsplitting volume.

Isabelle headed toward them, then stopped. She was floored, enough to drop her empty Yoo-hoo bottle and put a hand over her mouth.

One of the players, the tall one in the ratty yellow tank top and cutoff shorts, was Kenny Chesbro.

chapter 32

isabelle hadn't really expected to find Kenny. And she definitely hadn't expected that when she did, he'd run away from her.

But he did. He took one look at Isabelle—at her clothes, the way she was staring at him—and he took off around the back of the motel. His courtmates seemed flummoxed by this, though not enough to interrupt their game.

Isabelle, for her part, was shocked enough to hesitate. When she recovered her wits, she ran after him, her loafers sliding on the asphalt. Behind the motel the grass was overgrown, and as she plowed through it, one of her shoes fell off. She scrambled to find it, and when she stood back up, Kenny was nowhere in sight.

Where could he have gone? She ran around to the front of the motel, but he wasn't heading down the street. She thought he must've gone into the Dugout. So what could she do—knock on all the doors and hope he'd come out? Isabelle went around the back again, in case he'd decided to make a run for it across the empty field, but she didn't see him.

She was standing there weighing her options when she heard the gunshot.

And not just the bang; she also heard the bullet whiz past her head.

Isabelle dove for the dirt and stayed there. Apparently, that was the wrong thing to do.

"Go *away*," said a man's voice from inside the motel. It had to be Kenny; who else could it be? "Go away," he said again. "I mean it. Go away or I'll shoot."

She raised her head, but only long enough to answer.

"For chrissake," she said, "you're *already* shooting."

"Go *away*. Go away and leave me alone."

"Just listen, okay?" Isabelle said, trying to sound nonthreatening while yelling loud enough to be heard. "I'm not here to hurt you. I just want to talk."

He didn't answer. She wasn't sure, but she thought she heard a click that could've been the cocking of a gun.

"Kenny, please listen to me. My name's Isabelle Leonard. I work for Becky Belden Multimedia."

Another shot rang out, closer this time. She thought about yelling for help, but she doubted the hoopsters would hear her over the music; they sure didn't seem to have heard the shooting.

"Jesus *Christ*," she hollered, "I said I'm not here to hurt you. I just want to talk to you. I need to know what the hell's going on at BBM." No response. "Look, I know you're scared. They're trying to kill me, too. First some guy broke into my apartment and tried to electrocute me, okay? Then they poisoned my best friend and made it look like an overdose. And there've been others, lots of them. Please, you gotta believe me. Now, can I just come in there and talk to you?"

Her pleading speech was greeted with a pause so long she started to think he wasn't there anymore. But finally, he said, "How do I know you're telling the truth?"

"Because . . . I just am, okay?"

More silence. Then, "Stand up. Slow, okay? I mean it." She did as he asked. When she got to her feet, she saw the gun protruding from the torn screen of one of the motel windows. "Now put your hands up and keep 'em where I can see 'em."

For chrissake, she thought. *This guy watches more TV than I do.*

"Walk toward me," he ordered, sounding even more frightened than she was. "Not that fast. Wait—put your hands up higher."

She watched the gun barrel retreat from the window screen. Two seconds later the door opened. If she'd really been armed, she would've had plenty of time to draw her weapon and gun him down.

Kenny must've been steadying the barrel on the windowsill; once he was holding it in his hand, it was shaking like he had some localized palsy. Isabelle had been scared before, but now she was terrified that he really was going to shoot her, if only by accident.

"Would you please stop pointing that thing at me?"

He stopped in the doorway. "Why should I trust you?"

"Fine," she said, "you don't have to trust me. Just stop aiming that goddamn gun at me for five seconds. Please?" Warily, he dropped the revolver to his side. "Now, can we go inside and talk?"

"Out here's fine," he said. She realized he was scared to be alone with her, scared of what she might do to him if she got the chance. Even under the circumstances, the idea was almost funny.

"Fine," she echoed. "Can we at least sit down?"

He nodded. Outside each room was a rectangular concrete slab, the ruins of what used to be individual patios. Isabelle sat down on the edge, facing the scraggly grass. Her back was to him; she hoped he didn't decide to play it safe and blow her brains out.

Kenny also sat on the edge of the shallow slab, albeit ten feet away from her. He kept the gun in his hand, aimed at the empty field. He quelled the trembling by resting the gun on his knobby knees, long legs bent in a way that couldn't have been comfortable. From the way he was holding the weapon—at arm's length, like it was a snake that might bite him—Isabelle had a feeling he was even more afraid of it than she was.

"Why do you have a gun?" she asked.

"For protection."

"Well, thank you for not aiming it at me right now," she said.

He nodded. She remembered that on the TV show, his mother had said she'd brought her son up to be polite, especially to women.

"What do you want with me?"

She shook her head. "Honestly, I don't really know. I just . . . You were the only thing I could think of."

He nodded again. Then he looked her in the eye. "Is that true what you said just now? About somebody trying to kill you?"

"Yeah," she said. He made a noise that sounded to Isabelle like a sigh of relief, which threw her. "Is there a reason that makes you happy?"

"Oh, God, I'm sorry. It's just that . . . now I'm not the only one."

"What?"

"You've got no idea how lonely it is." There was a hollowness to his voice, like it was its own echo. "Just running, running, running, moving from one shitty town to another."

"What about all those people?" She pointed over his right shoulder, in the direction of the basketball game. The gesture seemed to spook him, and he tightened his grip on the pistol.

"Those guys kinda get to you after a while," he said once he'd breathed in and out a few times. "And besides, they're here because they wanna be. I've got no choice."

"So you've been on the road the whole time? Ever since you disappeared?"

"Disappeared?" The word didn't seem to taste good. "More like, since I ran for my fucking life."

His hands were shaking even harder. The urge to move closer, to comfort him, battled with the instinct not to get shot. He followed her gaze down to the gun, staring at the weapon like he suddenly wasn't quite sure where it'd come from.

"In school, I was big into the gun control thing," he said. His voice sounded empty, detached. "When I got this, I didn't even know how it worked. Guy had to show me. I can't even believe I'm holding this shit in my hand. It's amazing what a person'll do when they're terrified."

"I know," she said. She meant it.

"The goddamn thing scares the hell out of me, but I sleep with it under my pillow every night. I guess the only thing I'm more scared of than the gun is what I saw back at BBM."

"What happened?"

It was the question she'd been dying to put to him ever

since she first started to suspect he might still be alive. Now that she'd asked it, it hung in the air between them. He interested himself in the patch of dirt at the end of the concrete slab, poking at an old Clark bar wrapper faded almost to white. When he was done with that, he looked up at the sky. The clouds were congealed and grayish, like aging clam chowder.

"I worked in tech services. You knew that, right?" He waited for Isabelle's nod. "They were having all sorts of e-mail problems."

He paused, gazing out over the scraggly field. Isabelle wasn't sure whether to leave him alone or give him some encouragement.

"It wasn't by accident," he said after a while. "Somebody figured out how to get around the firewall—hacked into the system and let a worm loose, probably just a prank. And like I said, the e-mail server was screwed. A bunch of stuff wasn't getting delivered, and other stuff was getting sent like fifty times over. There were also problems with e-mail going to random people it hadn't really been sent to, and spam coming in disguised as messages from users in the company. It was a real mess. This went on for a couple of days, and, of course, everybody at tech serv was working like crazy."

Kenny suddenly stopped talking, his expression saying that he'd just remembered something. It turned out to be the fact that he had a pack of cigarettes in his pocket. They were a cheap generic brand, but he lit one and drew in the smoke like it was a pleasant surprise. He tucked the lighter inside the pack and started to put it back in his pocket. Then, as though he were remembering his manners, he extended the pack to Isabelle. Although she couldn't remember the last time she'd smoked tobacco, she nodded. He slid the pack along the concrete, still wary enough to keep his distance. She pulled the lighter out and lit a cigarette, the smoke burning its way down her lungs, nicotine giving her an instant head rush. It felt absolutely right. She slid the pack back to him, and he put it away.

"I was assigned to help figure out the spam thing," he continued, exhaling his own smoke in a long plume. "It was kind of a big deal, because it was pretty embarrassing for the company. Somebody had put together this porno picture of Becky—her head on some hot chick's body—and it was done up like an ad for an escort service. My boss was desperate to stop it from getting sent around any more than it already was, and looking like it was coming from people in BBM to boot."

He turned to Isabelle, as though to make sure she was still following him. She nodded.

"A lot of people still think e-mail is totally private, right? You send a message, and nobody gets to read it but the person you sent it to, and if you both delete it, it's gone forever."

"You mean it's not?"

"No way. First off, if you work for a company, law says your e-mail's their property. Some places, BBM included, you can't even send an e-mail with swearwords in it because the system'll reject it. Anyway, what I'm trying to tell you is that the company sets the rules and the system administrator enforces them. That means he can get in and look wherever he wants, do whatever he wants. Now, normally, nobody goes poking through other people's e-mails. It's not that interesting, and if you got caught, it'd get you fired. And most people like me don't have that kind of access, anyway—I'm way too far down the ladder. But during this whole mess, they gave temporary admin access to most of us in tech serv so we could try and clean it up.

"And that," he said, "is how it all started."

chapter 33

Kenny chewed on the last sentence, drawing it out. Isabelle could tell that the memory had been examined over and over, but that the frequency hadn't made it any easier to think about. She let him sit there awhile, dragging on his cigarette and looking out into nowhere.

"There were these e-mails," he said finally. "They were from some V.P., nobody I ever heard of. Now, normally, I wouldn't have been looking at somebody's mail, let alone someone that high up. In fact, the way things are set up at BBM, even the system administrator can't get in if you're one of the top people. There's a whole separate level of security for people like that.

"But like I said, everything was this huge disaster. This guy had spam flying out of his account like you wouldn't believe. So I was going through it all, trying to figure out what was crap I needed to show my boss so we could trace the hacker, versus what were real messages that ought to get sent on, when I came across these e-mails in his sent-mail folder."

He paused for another long drag on the cigarette. Finally, Isabelle couldn't stand it anymore.

"What did they say?"

His lips formed a grim smile. "At first, I thought it was a joke, you know? Like it was somebody's imaginary hit list—people who pissed you off at work or something. But then I realized it was for real."

"How?"

"I recognized a couple of the names. They were people at the company who'd actually died. And the dates on the e-mails—some of them were *before* these people croaked."

"So what did you do?"

"What do you think I did, lady? I totally freaked out. You wouldn't believe the shit I read. There was this one memo, talking about how important it was that the deaths all look like an accident. 'No suicides.' That's what it said. Quote, unquote. And there was this other e-mail toward the end with links to Web sites, and I clicked through to them. One was a story in the *Post* about how this girl died when she was pushed in front of a subway. Her name was on the list, too."

"Marcia Landon."

"Yeah. And then there were some facts and figures, stuff about a lot of money. I didn't understand it." He scratched at his scalp with both hands. Isabelle realized that at some point he'd put the gun down. She couldn't remember seeing him do it. "I didn't really want to understand it, I guess." He turned to her. "Listen, I'm not as dumb as I look."

"I never said you—"

"Hey, I dress like a bum. My mom tells me that every day. But I'm real good with computers, and I've got some street smarts, too. When I came across this stuff, I guess I knew I was in over my head. I had this instinct that if anybody found out I saw it, I was totally fucked."

"So you just ran?"

"No, not right that exact minute. At first, I tried to cover my tracks."

"How do you mean?"

He stood up. "You want a Coke?" She shook her head. "I could use a Coke."

He went into his room, taking the gun with him. He emerged a minute later, carrying a can still dripping from the cooler. The gun was nowhere in sight. He sat back down, only a yard of concrete between him and Isabelle. The can opened with a pop and a fizz, and he took a long swallow.

"Before anybody in tech serv can access a user's e-mail account, you always have to enter a password," he said. "And there's a record—it's one way of keeping people from snooping around. So after I found all that awful shit, I tried to fix it so nobody could see I'd been in there. But I couldn't figure out how to do it—not fast enough, anyway.

"And I don't know how they found out so quick, but the next thing I knew, all my access codes were revoked, even the low-level stuff I had before the hackers got in and messed everything up. And even though I know this is going to sound paranoid, I swear to God somebody tapped my phone—there was this weird clicking when you picked it up that wasn't there before." He shook his head. "You probably think I'm crazy."

"No, I don't," Isabelle said.

"I totally freaked out. I stayed until the end of the day, because what was I supposed to do? And when I went home, I could've sworn that somebody was following me. I was too scared to go in my building—it's a walk-up and the halls are really dark. So I just got on the subway and rode around all night. And in the morning, I couldn't make myself go to work. I just kept thinking about what I'd read on the Web. There was that girl who got pushed in the subway, and this guy who had a gas leak in his apartment, and somebody else who died because they picked the wrong kind of wild mushrooms. Can you believe that shit? And I kept thinking about what the e-mail said—how it had to look like an accident. And I thought if I stuck around, somebody was going to do that to me, too."

"So you took off without even telling your family?"

"I tried to tell them. I was afraid to call them because I thought maybe someone might be listening. So I hitchhiked to Green Bay, but there were strange cars in front of my parents' place and I got scared. And I thought about going to my friends, but I didn't want to drag them into it. By that time, I was pretty much terrified out of my mind. Every place I went I was looking over my shoulder. And I thought about going to Becky, but I was too scared. I just felt like I had to get the hell away."

"What made you want to go to her?"

"Because she didn't know anything about the murders."

"How could you be so sure?"

"One of the e-mails said that straight out. Said she was totally clueless, that she had no idea what was going on right under her nose at her own company. Said she was like a kid—she thought money grew on trees, or something like that. I don't remember it word for word."

"And who were they from?"

"What?"

"The e-mails. Who wrote them?"

"A vice president," he said, "named Maxwell Collins."

.　.　.

Later, Isabelle was amazed that she'd taken in the news without weeping. After all, it seemed eminently worth weeping over—the fact that Mac was in on the plot to kill BBM employees. Including her.

But was she really that shocked—really, down deep? Or had she always felt that she couldn't trust Mac, not even when his body was wrapped around hers? That night in the storage room, she'd thought one of the men moving the boxes sounded like Mac. She hadn't been certain, or even close to it, but it'd been enough to make her wary. And the whole time they'd been seeing each other, he'd always been distant, elusive. But he'd also seemed concerned about her; he'd even tried to get her to stay home from BBM. Now it looked as though the whole point of their relationship—of those fantastic New York Saturdays—had been to keep an eye on her.

Who the hell was Mac Collins? Had she really gone to bed with a murderer, seduced him with malice aforethought while he laughed at her behind her back? How naked had she actually been?

You need to take a hard look at the choices you're making.

That's what her sister had said. Even when they were kids, Margie had never had any respect for Isabelle's judgment. At the moment, neither did she.

The memory of that first night with Mac Collins flashed in front of her again, unwanted as a telemarketer. She'd known all along she wasn't sleeping with him for the right reasons, but it had felt so damn good. Now the thought of his hands on her made her feel sweaty, sad, sick to her stomach. Throwing up the pork rinds and Yoo-hoo on the bus back to Providence was a very real possibility, but at the moment, she was so miserable she didn't care.

She'd been unable to convince Kenny Chesbro to come back to New York with her, to tell what he knew so they could nail Mac and whoever his accomplices were. She'd tried for hours—taken him out for a beer and french fries at some scuzzy tavern, hit him with every argument she could think of. She told him that once he agreed to testify, the authorities would have to protect him, though she wasn't sure if that was even true. She tried explaining how much his family missed him, which only prompted him to beg her to get a message to his mom that he was okay.

Finally, he came up with what he thought was a reasonable compromise. He pulled out the old RadioShack cassette recorder he'd been using to chronicle the Klaw concert tour, and put his testimony on tape.

Hello, it began. *My name is Kenneth Chesbro. I was born in Green Bay, Wisconsin. I am twenty-two years old. Today is August the twenty-fifth. Two months ago I saw something in the Belden Building and it was so awful I ran for my life. I'm still running.*

The tape, nearly thirty minutes long, was tucked into the waistband of Isabelle's khakis; she was too nervous to leave it in her purse. She touched the hard plastic rectangle as she waited for the bus to Providence, which would take her to the train to New York, which would take her . . . where?

She'd thought about following Kenny's example and just running away, but she couldn't do it. Her heartsickness at learning the truth about Mac was hardening into anger, flowering into rage, and she was damned if she was just going to disappear. Wasn't that what he and his cohorts wanted—to get rid of her? So why should she do it for them?

But that left her with the question of what to do next. If she went to the police, would Kenny's tape be enough to convince them that she wasn't crazy?

The question occupied her so fully she barely noticed when the bus came. And when it did, she let it go—despite the fact that it was getting dark and she was already going to get back to the city after midnight.

The memory of all those TV crime dramas had convinced her that the tape wasn't enough. Wasn't there some legal rule that you couldn't get that kind of testimony admitted into evidence if the witness was available for cross-examination? She thought so; she had a vague memory of seeing something like that on *Law & Order*. She had to convince Kenny to come back with her, or at least she had to give it one last try.

The Dugout was deserted by the time she got back there. The Klaw Kids had departed for the eight o'clock show, and they seemed to be the motel's entire clientele. She went around to the back and knocked on Kenny's door, hoping he'd be in. He'd told her he was going to skip the concert; he wasn't in the mood.

There was no answer, which didn't surprise her. Kenny probably changed his mind, or went out to get something else to eat. Just to be sure, she tried to peek in the window, but the tattered curtain was drawn. Isabelle knew it hadn't been closed before—she remembered very well the image of the gun barrel sticking through the screen—and she wondered if he'd drawn it so he could get some rest.

She tried knocking again, more insistently, but there was no answer. So she tried the knob, and it turned, but the door still wouldn't budge.

It was locked from the inside.

Isabelle knocked louder, called Kenny's name. He still didn't answer.

She went back to the window and lifted the screen, starting at the screech of metal on metal. The wind had come up, and the curtain was billowing back into the room, partially blocking her view of the bed. She could see Kenny's legs, lying at what seemed to be an awkward angle, but when she yelled to him again, he still didn't respond.

She stretched an arm through the window and reached around to unlock the door. The Dugout Motel was not a high-security establishment.

She opened the door and found what was left of Kenny Chesbro.

chapter 34

Screaming is among the most primal of human instincts. The urge predates history, resides somewhere deep in the brain stem, has nothing at all to do with conscious thought.

So how horrifying must something be, Isabelle wondered later, to actually make you *forget* to scream?

But that was the only explanation she could think of for her silence on finding Kenny Chesbro. He was slumped on the bed, where he'd fallen after having the better part of his brain blown away from his body. That organ—gray, gelatinous, reddish purple—was running down the wall next to the bed.

Kenny's right hand still held the gun, the same one he'd aimed at Isabelle just hours before. On the nightstand was a spiral notebook, blue-lined paper right out of junior high. Scrawled on the open page were two words.

Sorry, Mom.

Kenny's eyes were wide open. Later, when she had the heart to think about it, she realized that those eyes were the first thing that told her this scene wasn't what it appeared to be—if she'd ever been inclined to believe it.

But the eyes didn't fit. She couldn't imagine, even in her fiction-obsessed mind, that a terrified young man who'd decided to end it all by putting a gun in his mouth and pulling the trigger wouldn't do it with his eyes squeezed shut. To keep your eyes open would be an act of bravery, and she didn't buy it.

And the eyes weren't the only thing. There was also everything she'd learned from Kenny in the past few hours—how desperately he wanted to live, how much he wanted to reassure his family that he was all right. He'd begged Isabelle to find a way to let them know he wasn't dead, that he'd come home as soon as he could. Besides, Isabelle knew her visit had given Kenny hope that he might be able to come out of hiding. The idea that he'd send Isabelle off to deliver the message, then end his life moments after she'd walked out the door, struck her as worse than ridiculous.

Isabelle didn't process all of this as she stood there in the horror movie that was Kenny's motel room. She barely stayed long enough for her mind to take in the scene in front of her. Then she fled out the door and around the building and down the street, running in loafers that were ill suited to anything more than a civilized trot.

. . .

It wasn't until the train was pulling into Penn Station that the truth occurred to her.

Whoever killed Kenny must've followed her to his motel room. Or to put it more brutally, she must've led him there.

For weeks, Kenny Chesbro had run for his life. The people

who'd been killing BBM employees—Mac, his accomplices, whomever they employed to do their dirty work—had searched for him, to no avail. Then, through luck and some common sense, she'd found him. And she'd killed him, as surely as if she'd shoved the gun into his mouth and pulled the trigger.

It was her fault that Kenny was dead. But not just him. She was almost positive that the drug that killed Trevor had been meant for her. If Kenny and Trevor had never met her, they'd still be alive.

What could she do now? Where could she go?

She thought about her few haunts in the city—her apartment, the Cosmo. Where could she go that might be safe? She knew that if she showed up on their doorstep, Mr. and Mrs. Mendes would take her in. But how could she put them in danger? Even going to her sister's in California was out of the question now. She couldn't risk letting anything happen to the twins, the niece and nephew she'd never even met.

She hailed a cab outside Penn Station, too scared to take the subway this late. Indecision was leading her home.

Before she went into her building, she asked the doorman to escort her upstairs. Her apartment was both empty and undisturbed.

Hands shaking, she poured herself a drink from the bottle of Knob Creek. She carried it through the apartment as she double-checked the locks on the windows, even the ones that were five stories up and nowhere near a fire escape.

Maybe she'd never leave the apartment again. Maybe she'd stay there forever, doors barred against the world—against strangers, evicting landlords, and especially the evil bastards who wanted her dead.

But why hadn't they killed her yet? Surely, they'd had chances, even more than the two times they'd already tried. Was there some reason they'd left her alive?

She finished her drink and poured another. She wasn't used to whiskey, not in great gulps like this, and the liquid burned its way down just like the cigarette she'd smoked with Kenny Chesbro.

The thought of Kenny made her start to sob, but the tears wouldn't come. She ran into her bedroom and threw herself on the futon, suffering the crying version of dry heaves. The bed still smelled like Mac Collins.

Mac. How could she have been so stupid? Was it really possible that in the space of a year she'd let herself be deceived *twice*? Both men had pretended to care for her—Laurence for reasons of his own ego, Mac so he could get away with murder. The realization that all those lovely New York days had been nothing more than a way to keep an eye on her made her cry so hard she found herself gasping for air.

When the sobbing finally passed, she took out her old Sports Walkman. Then, in an act of penance her Catholic mother would have understood, she put in Kenny's tape and pushed Play. She listened to it, all of it, and when she was done, the tears came in force.

But they didn't come alone. They came with regret and fear and a white-hot desire for vengeance.

And an idea.

chapter 35

The dressing room was everything Isabelle had imagined. It had plush sofas with brightly striped slipcovers cinched in perfect bows, and riots of flowers, and a china tea service in the corner. On a low glass-topped coffee table was a crystal candy dish overflowing with imported licorice; in the center of the long lighted dressing table was a giant bowl of potpourri, calming the room with the scents of rosemary and lavender.

Isabelle thought it was charming—and a strange setting for what she had to do, which was break Becky Belden's heart.

She'd never been in Becky's personal dressing room before; she'd been too far down on the totem pole even to be allowed to freshen the flowers in the sanctum sanctorum. But she knew where it was, of course. And when she learned that Becky was on the set shooting episodes of *Becky Belden's Food 'n' Friends*—not in her penthouse office, not in her Gramercy Park brownstone, not out at Shelby's Landing—the dressing room was where she had to go.

If Isabelle's mind had been on her work, she would've known where to look for Becky; the *Food 'n' Friends* shoot had been scheduled for weeks. But *The Becky Belden Show* and its spin-offs had been the least of her concerns, and now any thoughts of future employment seemed asinine. She hadn't even reported to work that morning, had snuck into the studio and gone straight to Becky's dressing room. The first show was just getting started, and as she'd made her way backstage, she'd heard a voice that nearly made her turn and run out.

"So, folks, are you ready to watch Becky whip up some special Italian desserts? I hope you are, because Becky's guest today is Enzo Antonioni from Enzo's restaurant right here in New York City. Enzo's going to teach Becky how to make cannoli, pizzelli, biscotti, tiramisu, and a very special tartufo. Becky tells me that when the holidays come around, this could be the perfect way to spice up your table with a taste of Italy! She'll be taking calls from her friends at home and offering samples to some lucky members of the studio audience, so she hopes you'll enjoy spending the next hour with her. The show will get started in about fifteen minutes, and to get you in the mood, we'll be serving espresso, compliments of our good friends at Roma Coffee . . ."

It was Mac Collins, warming up the crowd. She flattened herself against the wall, terrified that he could see her. He looked so friendly and open, so deceptively preppy and upbeat. But what did she expect him to do—stand in front of the crowd wearing a T-shirt that said I AM A MISERABLE MURDERING SON OF A BITCH?

She got to Becky's dressing room without running into anyone. She knocked, and a voice told her to come in. Isabelle opened the door, praying that it would be Becky, and that she'd be alone.

It was, and she was. The makeup artist must've just left, because Becky still had tissues protruding from her collar like a lion's mane. She was standing in front of the mirror with a sheet of paper, as though she'd been practicing a speech. When Isabelle got close enough, she'd find it contained a list of Italian words: *delizioso, buon gusto, mangia.*

"Isabelle," Becky said, surprised but not perturbed. "I'm glad to see you're feeling better."

Isabelle had no idea what she was talking about; the fact that she'd called in sick the day before had fled her memory. "I need to talk to you," she said.

"Something about the show?" Becky was smiling at her; it was an expression Isabelle had seen on her face many times, like a benevolent queen with her lady-in-waiting. "I hope Enzo hasn't been pestering the P.A.'s," she said. "The man's a genius in the kitchen, but he can't keep his hands to himself."

"That's not it," Isabelle said. "It's not the show. It's something else. Something about BBM. Something awful." The words were coming out in a cascade, a stream of consciousness that Isabelle couldn't control. Even as she spoke, part of her knew she sounded like a mental patient.

"Are you sure you're all right?" Becky squinted at her, the heavy makeup caking around her eyes. "Why don't you just—"

"*Now,*" Isabelle said. "I have to talk to you *now.*"

"Do you realize that we're on live in—"

"Someone's been killing the people who work for you," she said. "I know it's going to sound crazy, but there's some kind of a conspiracy to kill BBM employees. Lisa Kinne. Marcia Landon. Trevor Hopkins. There's at least eight of them, and I don't know how many more. And Kenny Chesbro. I found him in Rhode Island yesterday, and he told me everything. I've got it all on tape." She pulled the cassette out of her pocket. "And then after he talked to me, someone killed him. They tried to make it look like a suicide, but it wasn't."

Becky stood still, the paper still suspended in midair. "You found Kenny Chesbro? How did you—"

"He was on the run because of some e-mails he saw. They talked about the whole plan, the different ways of killing people. And he told me"—Isabelle's mouth was having a hard time forming the words—"he told me they were written by Mac Collins. He's the one who's behind the whole thing. And Kenny—he wanted to go to you, but he was too scared. He just kept running, and he was fine until I found him, and then—" Isabelle could feel the tears start to come back, but she shook them off. "I know this all sounds crazy, but you have to believe me. We have to stop him. I thought about going to the police, but I don't have enough proof. But you can get it. And they'll have to believe you. I mean . . . you're *Becky Belden*."

Becky's hand went to her throat; she looked like a heroine in a Victorian novel. For a second, Isabelle thought she might actually faint; her knees looked in danger of buckling. But she made it to the round ottoman, covered in the same colorful stripes as the couches. The furniture might've come from a very tasteful circus, and in her present state, Isabelle found its festive air oppressive.

"Dear God," Becky said. The way it came out, it sounded like a genuine prayer. "Tell me . . . tell me everything."

Isabelle told her the whole story, starting with the day she'd found Marcia Landon's photo in her desk and ending with the horrific scene in Kenny Chesbro's motel room. Becky listened in silence, seeming so shell-shocked Isabelle wondered if she was taking it all in.

"You poor girl," Becky said when she'd finished. "I wish you'd come to me sooner."

"I didn't know what to do," Isabelle said. "I was so scared. And I was all by myself."

Becky reached for her hand. "You're not alone any—"

"Five minutes to air. Becky to the set, please." The intercom's disembodied voice made them both jump.

"The show," Becky said.

"What are you going to do?"

Becky shook her head, as though it might help her think more clearly. "I have to go on," she said finally. "Just stay here and wait for me." She stood up, looked in the mirror, took a deep breath. Then she gave Isabelle her best Becky Belden smile. "And have some tea," she said. "It'll do you good."

Isabelle did as she was told. She wasn't thirsty, but pouring the tea gave her something to do with her hands. She took it to the love seat, where she watched the show on the monitor. The chef was teaching Becky how to wrap dough around metal tubes and deep-fry them to make cannoli shells, punctuating the lesson by singing snippets of Italian love songs. Becky gamely mixed the sugar and ricotta for the filling, singing along as though she hadn't a care in the world—as though she hadn't just learned that her company was rotting from the inside.

Isabelle was contemplating Becky's composure, thinking that it was something superhuman, when the door opened without so much as a knock. And before she could yell for help, she found herself locked in a soundproof room with Mac Collins.

chapter 36

isabelle gasped, stood up, ran as far away from Mac as she could. It seemed to confuse him. He came toward her, and she grabbed the closest thing she could find to defend herself. It was Becky's china teapot, and she hurled it at him with all her strength. The action took him by surprise; he didn't have time to duck. The teapot struck him square in the chest, spewing amber liquid over his shirtfront before hitting the carpeted floor.

"What the—"

"Help! Somebody help me!"

Her panicked screams filled the room, seeming to bounce off the mirrors and multiply. Mac advanced on her; she tried to retreat farther, but the wall didn't budge.

"Get away from me!"

"Isabelle, for chrissake, it's me. I'm here to help you. Jesus, I just want to get you out of here. What the hell were you thinking of, coming—"

"I *know*. I know everything, you son of a bitch. I know what you did to those people. And I've got *proof*."

"What the hell are you talking about?"

"Kenny Chesbro." Just the name was enough to make her start crying; this time she couldn't stop. "I found him. He told me everything. He told me how he accidentally read those e-mails you wrote, about your plot to kill all those people. Jesus Christ, I am such an *idiot*. I'm spilling my guts to you, letting you screw me no less, and you're laughing at me behind my back."

He closed the distance between them and grabbed her shoulders so tightly she could picture the precise shape of the bruises to come. "Listen to me," he said through clenched teeth. "I did *not* write any e-mails. I am *not* the one responsible for all this. It's Becky."

"That is the most disgusting—"

"It's true. I swear. Listen to me, Isabelle. We don't have a lot of time. Becky's going to get off the air in a couple of minutes. You've got to tell me what you said to her."

She glared at him. "You're a goddamn lying bastard. Becky would never—"

He shook her so hard the back of her head hit the wall. "You have to trust me," he said. "You know how hard I've been working. I've been trying to figure out where the hell all the money's coming from. By every damn financial principle I ever learned, the company ought to be in dire straits. But there's millions of dollars coming in. It's what's keeping the place in the black, making it look profitable. It wasn't until you told me about the deaths of all those employees that I finally figured it out."

Over his shoulder, the monitor showed Becky Belden and an elderly Chinese lady from the studio audience piping cannoli filling into the shells with a pastry bag. The woman laughed as hers overflowed, the creamy ricotta mixture exploding out of the pastry like toothpaste from a tube. Becky's, by contrast, ended in a perfect rosette. The audience clapped. The theme music swelled.

"Please, Isabelle," he said. "I have to get you out of here. It's only a matter of time until Becky figures out how much you know."

"She already knows." She spat the words at him. "I already told her. She's going to take care of everything. She's going to make sure that you never—"

"For chrissake, what do I have to gain? It's not my company. What do you think, that I'm having people killed for a few extra stock options?"

"I don't believe you."

"Fine," he said. "Don't believe me. You can accuse me of anything you want. Just please come with me."

"I . . ." Her voice trailed off. She had no idea what to do. Could Mac be telling the truth? His expression was so pleading, his voice so rock-solid earnest. But then she thought about Kenny, how he'd told her Becky was innocent and Mac was guilty. It was one of the last things he'd ever said; it had to be true.

"Get away from me," she said. "I fell for your nice-guy crap once. I'm not going to do it again."

"Isabelle, please—"

Becky walked in. Even her well-bred composure couldn't mask her shock at seeing Mac Collins with his hands on Isabelle.

"Get away from her," she said, taking a few steps toward them. "Isabelle, are you all right? Did he hurt you?"

"Call the police," Isabelle said.

Becky nodded and picked up the phone. "This is Becky Belden speaking. There's a dangerous man backstage at my television studio. He's threatening to take a woman hostage. Please come immediately." She gave the address and hung up.

Mac shook his head in what looked to Isabelle like disgust. "Just drop the act," he said. "I know what you've been doing, you and your cronies on the top floor. I know all about it. So does Isabelle. And pretty soon, so will the feds."

Becky's expression was all confusion and outrage. "You're the one who needs to stop pretending," she said. "Isabelle tells me you've been up to some terrible things. You've betrayed people who trusted you, who considered you a friend. And I understand she has proof."

"If there's any so-called proof, it's because you concocted it to make me the fall guy. What, did you need someone to pin it on if you ever got caught?"

Becky's mouth fell open. "You twisted, evil man."

"For chrissake, stop trying to sound like someone's tied you to the train tracks. I know what you've been up to."

"What are you—"

"Tell her," he barked. "Tell her about the insurance." Becky didn't answer. "For chrissake, tell her about the 'dead peasants' insurance."

Isabelle wasn't sure she'd heard him right. "Dead . . . peasants?"

"Tell her why they call it that," he said to Becky. When she didn't respond, he turned back to Isabelle. "It's because, to the queen, the peasants are worth more dead than alive."

"I don't know what you're talking about," Becky said.

"It's a dirty little secret even some people in the insurance business know nothing about," he said. "Becky here took it to what you'd call an absurd extreme."

Isabelle looked to Becky, whose face was still a mixture of concern and confusion.

"A company can take out life insurance policies on its employees," Mac continued. "Lots of firms do it, to compensate for the cost of hiring and training a replacement. It's all perfectly legal—it's right there in the stack of paperwork you sign when you start a new job. And for some companies, it makes for a tidy little windfall. I read in the *Wall Street Journal* once where a chain of record stores collected a quarter million dollars for a minimum-wage salesclerk who died of AIDS. But Becky here . . . she saw it as operating capital. She did business with insurance companies all over the world, to make good and sure nobody figured out what she was up to."

The woman in question took a step closer. "Isabelle, get away from him," she said. "The police will be here soon."

"You didn't call the cops." He turned to Isabelle. "There's no way she called the cops. Not when she was preying on her own employees, taking advantage of weak, lonely people who trusted her. You were the one who pointed it out to me, Isabelle—how all the people who died had no close family. That's because she needed people who wouldn't be missed, who didn't leave anyone behind who'd ask too many questions.

"And what was the point? Oh, sure, it was money. You need lots of it to run a company as your own personal vanity project, hiring your own little coterie of groupies because they amuse you or flatter your almighty vanity. You decorate the place like it's the goddamn Taj Mahal—and God forbid Becky Belden has to sell off one of her prize racehorses to pay the bills. But it wasn't just about money, was it? It was also because you liked playing the benevolent goddess, having the power of life and death. Never mind just hiring and firing—the great Becky giveth and she taketh away."

Becky's jaw was so tight Isabelle thought the muscles might snap. "Are you finished?"

"Not even close. But the rest of my talking I'm doing to the FBI and the SEC. They'll be very damn interested in what you've been doing to manipulate earnings in advance of the IPO, not to mention money laundering and murder." He turned to Isabelle. "Now do you believe me?"

She looked from him to Becky and back again. She didn't know what to think. Becky had been so kind to her—and she seemed so filled with righteous indignation—that Isabelle couldn't believe she could be guilty. But Mac seemed equally sincere. Whom was she supposed to trust?

"Come on," he said. "I'm getting you out of here."

He grabbed her arm. Becky blocked his way.

"Don't go with him, Isabelle," she said. "God only knows what he'll do if he gets you alone."

Their wills were equally strong. Mac, however, had seven inches and sixty pounds on her. He pushed Becky out of the way and dragged Isabelle toward the door. Her indecision made for halfhearted resistance.

They were halfway to the door when it opened, then closed again.

Standing in front of it was the man who'd invaded Isabelle's apartment. The man who'd been following her. The man who'd tried to kill her.

And he was holding a gun.

chapter 37

The man's appearance had a transformative effect on both women. Isabelle shrieked and took two steps backward. Becky took an equal number of steps forward, in the direction of the door.

"Finally," she said.

It was one word, three syllables, but it contained Becky Belden's transformation from domestic goddess to . . . Isabelle wasn't sure what. For the moment, all she could assess were the outward signs—and they were something amazing. Isabelle could've sworn that Becky's voice was lower, her back straighter, her eyes colder. If she had still been working on her sci-fi novel, she would've said that Becky Belden had just morphed into her evil twin—as it turned out, her foulmouthed evil twin.

"What the fuck took you so long?"

The man stood in front of the closed door. His smile was one of quiet satisfaction. Isabelle looked from him to Becky—the new Becky, the nasty, evil, untrustworthy Becky—and then to Mac. She felt as though she'd been drop-kicked through the rabbit hole.

"You called him," Isabelle said into the silence. "When you said you called the police, you really called him. Didn't you?"

"No," Becky said. There was nothing reassuring in her voice, which made Isabelle think she was telling the absolute truth. "Collins was right. When I said I was calling the police, I wasn't calling anyone."

"Then—"

"I called my friend here the minute I walked out of the dressing room. Imagine my discontent when I came back to find you not only still here but still *alive*, and in the company of my favorite vice president."

"Mac was telling the truth," Isabelle said. "It was you all along."

Becky smiled and clapped her hands, like Isabelle had seen her do on TV when one of her guests managed to flip an omelet without spilling it onto the burner.

"Give the girl a fucking prize," she said. "What shall we give her? Ah, I know. A memorial service. A lovely one, filled with flowers and singing and catered refreshments. Perhaps I'll say a few words myself: Poor Isabelle," she said in a singsong voice that Isabelle found profoundly creepy, "jilted at the altar, only to have her heart broken again by another awful man. Who could blame her for killing him and then taking her own life? And right here, backstage on *The Becky Belden Show*. Clearly, the poor girl just snapped . . ."

Becky seemed to be enjoying herself. So did the man with the gun. Mac Collins looked like he would've dearly loved to strangle them both. Isabelle, for her part, was speechless. How do you respond to your own eulogy?

"I have to say, Isabelle, you turned out to be one fourteen-karat pain in the ass." She'd dropped both the fake smile and the creepy voice and gone back to being merely evil. "Because your sorry little tale amused me, I gave you the cushiest job in the company, working for a moron like Lisa Kinne—and you wouldn't even do me the courtesy of letting my magazine do a story on you. Such *ingratitude*.

"And the next thing I know, you're sticking your nose into my business, asking around about Marcia Landon. What choice did I have but to bring you over to the TV show so I could keep an eye on you? At least you turned out to be an ideal candidate for my little income-generating program. But then you had the perfectly awful manners to just *refuse* to die. You somehow managed to thwart the best contract killer money can buy." She gave the blond man a withering look. "You're supposed to be the best, but you can't manage to get rid of a little hick who can barely navigate the goddamn subway."

"Becky, one minute, please. Becky to the set, please. We're on live in fifty-five seconds."

The announcement didn't faze Becky in the least. She turned to the mirror and checked her makeup, speaking to her own reflection. "Well, I have to go," she said. "Live television waits for no one. And I just adore a good tartufo, don't you?" She walked toward the door, stopping in front of the man with the gun. "You know what to do," she said. "And for heaven's sake, get it right this time." She stepped around him, then paused with her hand on the doorknob.

"Oh," she said over her shoulder, "and while I still have the chance, there's something I've been wanting to say."

She smiled, the delight on her face much, much scarier than the sarcasm.

"Go to hell, Isabelle," she said.

. . .

The three of them just stood there for a moment, as awkward as new acquaintances at a bad party. Isabelle was still in shock over Becky's transformation from benevolent aunt to cast-iron bitch. Mac, who had edged his body between her and the other man, seemed to have a healthy respect for the gun.

"Let Isabelle go," Mac told him. "This can be between just you and me."

The blond-haired man laughed, like he'd just heard the mother of all jokes.

Then he shot him in the chest.

Isabelle gasped as Mac crumpled to the floor, the expression on his face one of intense confusion. She took a step toward him, but the other man stopped her.

"Don't do that," he said in a tone that sounded strangely like he was warning her off from something that might hurt her. "Stay away from him."

She watched the red stain expand across the front of Mac's shirt. He was struggling for breath, staring at some spot four feet in front of where she was standing. Isabelle had never seen anyone get shot before, not in real life, but she was pretty sure he was going to die.

She took another step toward him, but the blond-haired man just said, "No."

"Why did you do that?" she asked.

She wasn't sure why she said it; even as the words came out, she knew it was a moronic question.

"It's what I do," he said.

She turned to face him. He was still holding the gun, now pointed straight at her.

"I'm next, aren't I?"

He smiled at her again, then came toward her. Isabelle braced herself for the gunshot. Would she hear it before it hit? She had no idea what it would feel like; maybe it would be over so fast she wouldn't feel it at all.

He kept walking until they were face-to-face. Up close, he looked younger than she'd thought when she'd seen him on the street, younger than when she'd served him in the diner. His eyes were very pale blue, his hair wavy and sun-bleached. He looked so *normal*, so all-American. If she'd met him in Burlington, she would've thought he was a grad student in some practical field, like mechanical engineering.

He came so close Isabelle could no longer see the gun; she imagined it must be an inch from her body, aimed at some vital organ. With his left hand, he stroked the top of her head, sliding his hand down her cheek, then her shoulder, her upper arm. Isabelle was too scared to do anything but stand still.

"You were my first," he said.

The words hung in the air for a few seconds before Isabelle managed to speak.

"The first . . . person you ever tried to kill?"

She felt him laugh against her hair. "Oh, no. There have been a lot of those. No, you were something much more important. You were the first one who got away."

"*'Biscotti' means twice-cooked. So Chef Enzo's going to show us how baking our chocolate-dipped hazelnut amaretto biscotti two times will make them nice and crunchy. First we start by mixing the dry ingredients, which I like to do by hand with this big wooden spoon . . .*"

It was Becky's latest cooking lesson, piped in on the monitor behind Isabelle. She sounded as friendly and perky as ever; there was no trace of the homicidal sociopath of a few minutes ago.

"You're very special to me, Isabelle," the man was saying. "Until you, it was all about business." She didn't know what to say. "I'm very good at my job, you know. I was the one Becky called in after my colleague botched Marcia Landon and I had to clean up his mess. Since then, I've had her exclusive contract." He leaned down and whispered into her ear. "Becky only wants the best."

"You're the one who pushed her in front of the train."

Isabelle hadn't meant it as a question. Neither had she meant it as a compliment. That, however, is how he took it.

"I was quite proud of that one." He ran a finger along her jawbone. "Monitor her e-mail, find out about a late-night movie date. Then wait until just the right moment, when nobody's watching but some inebriated old bum who makes the perfect patsy. It's all about planning. Getting to know your subject until she feels like an old friend, like a lover." The man buried his face in Isabelle's hair and drew in a deep breath, as though she were the bowl of lavender and rosemary on Becky's vanity. "But you," he said, "are something more."

"Now, I've talked on several occasions about the importance of using real vanilla. I know it's more expensive than the artificial kind, but trust me, it's worth it! Later on, we're going to show you how wonderful it is to cook with freshly grated nutmeg . . ."

Isabelle wanted to push him away, but the gun in her abdomen made her quell the instinct. "What do you want from me?"

He ignored her so thoroughly she had the feeling he hadn't even heard her. "You made me sloppy," he said. "From the first time I saw your file, you distracted me. I never even thought to check how the outlets in your bathroom were wired, and that was before we ever even met. The way you ran downstairs after me, dripping wet, completely naked . . . *amazing*. But I shouldn't have expected anything less from a woman who had the guts to go alone to her own wedding reception."

He ran a hand over her breast and took a step closer, until their bodies touched. In a wave of fear and revulsion, Isabelle realized that he had an erection.

"And then in the club, when that Neanderthal propositioned you, you tossed a drink in his face. And you never drank your cocktail, after I went to all the trouble of spiking it with Rohypnol." He smiled at the memory. "It would've been such a clever method, too. You wouldn't have been the first girl accidentally poisoned by some would-be rapist. But then your friend drank it instead. It was as though God himself didn't want me to carry out my contract, wanted me to let you live so we could be together. Isn't that remarkable?"

He seemed to want an answer. Isabelle had no idea what to say.

chapter 38

The man had killed Trevor. He'd just admitted it, and he seemed no more perturbed than if he were copping to some minor social faux pas. Her throat constricted so tightly she was afraid she was going to lose the ability to breathe. The blond man's smile grew wider, though it never reached his eyes.

"And then there was Kenny Chesbro. Becky spent a fortune trying to track him down, but I may never have found him if it weren't for you. And just think—if I'd done my job successfully that night in your apartment, I never would've been able to complete that contract. By surviving, you made Kenny's death possible. Don't you just love the irony?"

Finally, Isabelle had enough. *Let him shoot me,* she thought; anything was better than standing there while Mac bled to death, his killer pawing her like they were slow-dancing at the junior prom.

"You sick son of a bitch," she said. "Do you actually not get that you're the bad guy?"

He laughed and kissed her gently on the cheek. "Right and wrong are so bourgeois," he said. "I'm an artist. I'm like Shakespeare or Michelangelo. Or maybe I should say I'm Dante; I seem to recall that you like to read him, don't you?"

"How the hell do you—"

"My point, lovely Isabelle, is that when you're as good as I am, you're exempt from that sort of tiresome morality. How many people in the world know that viral meningitis can be used as a murder weapon? That one could acquire the correct sample and inject it using the tiniest of needles while the victim is sleeping in his own bed? Isn't that brilliant? In its own way, isn't it poetry?"

"Then we fold in the whole hazelnuts. It's never good to overmix the dough, is it, Chef Enzo? Now watch how he's forming it into two neat logs, which he'll bake at three hundred fifty degrees for fifteen minutes. Now, to save time, we're going to pull this completed batch out of the oven. Don't they smell scrumptious?"

The blond man leaned in again to whisper in her ear. "Have you been enjoying your laptop? Creating your literary masterpiece?"

"I threw it into the river."

She could feel his smile. "I don't think you did any such thing. In fact, I doubt that knowing it came from me made it any less valuable. Perhaps much, much more."

"Why would you even—" She cut herself off. Just having a conversation with him suddenly felt perverse.

"Why would I send it to you?" He paused, as though he hadn't actually considered the question before. "To atone for my sins. After all, I'm not a thief. I took it because it was necessary. I had to make it look like a burglary after I failed to execute my contract that night in your apartment. But then I realized that I had a piece of you in my hands—your thoughts, your stories, even your e-mail. I owed you something in return."

"You sick—"

He leaned in closer. "I wanted you to know that I was following you. I let you catch me. You knew that, didn't you?"

"Yes," she said through a clenched jaw.

"And how did that make you feel?"

She took in half a breath. "Like I was being chased by some crazy bastard who was trying to kill me."

Her answer, like so many other things, seemed to strike him as funny.

"Well," he said, "you're half right."

She never got a chance to find out which half he was talking about. The door opened again, and in walked Bill Friedrich—BBM's director of corporate communications, the one who'd been nice enough to call to make sure she was okay when Lisa died, who hadn't made a fuss when she spilled coffee on his shirt.

Isabelle's heart leaped with the hope that the cavalry had arrived. It sank just as quickly.

"For chrissake," Friedrich said, "haven't you killed her yet?"

. . .

The blond man backed away from Isabelle, though only a step. "What are you doing here?"

"Becky sent me to make sure you'd wrapped things up," he said. "Which I see that you haven't."

"Don't tell me how to do my job."

"Jesus," Friedrich said, "they're going to a commercial in another"—he looked at his watch—"five and a half minutes.

Becky's going to come in and find them both. So come on, get it over with."

"Don't," the man repeated slowly, "tell me how to do my job."

The menace in his voice made Friedrich raise both hands in a posture of surrender. "Fine, fine. I'm not the one who's got to answer to Becky if it doesn't go the way it's supposed to."

The blond man's smile got almost imperceptibly tighter. "Do you honestly think," he said, "that I answer to anyone?"

The question was still hanging in the air when the door opened again. Even in her present state of abject terror, it occurred to Isabelle that she'd stumbled into some bizarre drawing room comedy.

The new arrival was Jeffrey Bing, the human resources vice president—the short-tempered one whom Isabelle had considered the bad cop to Friedrich's good. In the half second after he walked in, she entertained the hope that *he* might be her knight in shining armor; since Becky and Bill Friedrich had turned out to be evil, maybe Bing was a good guy, after all.

No such luck. Rather than being outraged at the sight of Mac bleeding to death at the feet of a gun-wielding stranger, he just seemed exasperated.

"Come on," he said. "Are you going to kill her or aren't you?"

The blond man turned his pale blue eyes on Jeffrey Bing. In the ensuing silence, Isabelle thought she heard Mac moan in pain. "I think," the man said, "that the two of you should leave."

"Come off it," Bing said. "Becky hired you to do a job, and she's paying you top dollar. I wired it to your goddamn offshore account myself, so I'm well aware of what a top-end contract killer is earning these days." He walked over to Mac and examined him, noting his shallow breathing like he was reading the ticker on a penny stock. "You know the drill. Collins here will be gonzo in a minute, then you pop her in the head so it looks like she did it herself, same as Chesbro. Bullets get planted in her desk along with the suicide note. So stop acting like a lovesick schoolboy and get it over with."

Isabelle watched the man's grip tighten on the gun. She had no idea whether it was because he was about to shoot Bing—or her.

"Let's just calm down," Friedrich said. "Once Collins and the girl are out of the picture, everything'll go on just like before."

Isabelle took a baby step toward the door, hoping the three of them were too preoccupied to notice. The blond man smiled at her, shaking his head like he was correcting a naughty child. She stepped back.

"Becky's got a solid plan. All we have to do is—" Friedrich stopped short, as though he'd heard something strange. "All we—"

He stopped again, turning to stare at the monitor. On the set of *Food 'n' Friends*, Becky and her guests were clustered at the kitchen counter, the ingredients for tiramisu arrayed in front of them. But no one was cooking. They were just standing there, looking like they were driving past a car wreck.

Bing took a step toward the monitor. "What the hell?"

His voice echoed back to him through the television. He and Friedrich stared at it in confusion, then looked around the room.

"It's Collins," Friedrich said. "He turned on his goddamn body mike."

He strode over to where Mac lay, ripping the black wire off the front of his shirt. The ensuing electronic shriek filled both the dressing room and the TV studio. Friedrich tossed the radio mike and its attached battery pack onto the carpet, then looked at Bing. His eyes were wide, skin even whiter than usual.

"Show goes out live on the Food Network," Friedrich said.

Bing slammed a fist into his palm. "Son of a *bitch*." He strode over to Mac and kicked him squarely in the side. Isabelle heard him groan, but even from where she was standing, she thought she saw him smile.

On the set, Chef Enzo and a middle-aged woman pulled from the studio audience were staring at each other, mouths agape. And as for Becky Belden: she seemed frozen, like she'd become her own likeness at Madame Tussaud's, the egg she'd been about to break suspended in midair over a large ceramic bowl.

She dropped it, and it fell to the floor with a crack. Without a word, she turned and ran off the set, her own body mike broadcasting the fall of her footsteps. The screen cut to a slate that said, EXPERIENCING TECHNICAL DIFFICULTIES.

"Jesus *Christ*," Bing said. "What do we do now?" Then he looked around the room. "Jesus *Christ*," he said again, "where the hell did he go?"

Isabelle, like the others, had been transfixed by the TV monitor. Now the urgency in Bing's voice made her turn around.

The man with the gun had vanished.

chapter 39

isabelle hated hospitals. She knew she wasn't alone in this, but she was convinced that she hated them more than most people did. She'd logged countless hours there when her parents were dying, almost exactly two years apart; she'd sat under flickering fluorescent lights and eaten stale sandwiches while the doctors made her parents feel even worse than the cancer had. She'd never entered a hospital to visit a sick friend or admire a new baby, and she didn't understand people who did.

But what could she do when Mac was in surgery and her own stupidity had put him there? She had to go, despite the fact that the fancy urban trauma center seemed just as depressing as the hospital back home. One was in New York City, the other in northeastern Vermont, but the places even *smelled* the same.

It didn't help that in the waiting room the ancient TV set was tuned to CNN, and there was no way to change the channel. The network was offering coverage of exactly one story: the

Becky Belden scandal. It was showing the footage of the live broadcast in what seemed like an endless loop—Becky happily making dessert, the disembodied voices arguing over her plans for a double homicide, her dropping the egg and fleeing the studio.

Although her press office had issued a statement calling the situation "a practical joke gone horribly wrong," the police were looking for her. The fact that Mac had been shot in the chest in her dressing room made her, as the NYPD had delicately put it, "a person of interest."

So far, there was no sign of her. Friedrich and Bing, however, had been intercepted at JFK, with plane tickets to Belize and two fake passports. It was something of an out-of-body experience to watch the past several hours of her life relayed through the grainy set—how the hit man had shot Mac and slipped away without a trace, how Bing and Friedrich had fled the moment they realized they'd been left holding the bag, how Isabelle had run into the packed TV studio screaming for someone to call 911.

She turned away from the television, wishing she could mute the volume. The author of a Becky Belden biography was chronicling how she'd risen from humble origins to the height of wealth and fame; both her voice and the subject matter were aggravating Isabelle's headache.

"As a teenager, Belden ran the household for her widowed father, raising two younger sisters on his bus driver's salary. But even though money was tight, she always made sure they had a few special touches to brighten their lives . . ."

Isabelle went to the coffee machine and bought herself another cup of the hospital's putrid brew. The caffeine and the guilt were the only things keeping her conscious.

Back in the waiting room, one patient's family was dug in for the long haul: bags of chips, liters of soda, a big box from Krispy Kreme. They'd offered her a doughnut, and she'd forced herself to eat it. It was the first thing she'd had all day.

She wandered down the hall, wondering if Mac's family was going to show up. She figured someone at the hospital must've notified them, or maybe someone from BBM; shouldn't their contact information be in his personnel file?

And what would she say to them if they did come? *Hi, I'm Isabelle. I'm sleeping with your son. And by the way, I'm the one who almost got him killed.*

She was busy imagining the scene when someone grabbed her from behind. He clamped his hand over her mouth so quickly and firmly she didn't even have a chance to scream.

·   ·   ·

She felt herself being pulled backward through a door, and though she struggled to get free, his grip on her was iron-clad. The next thing she knew, she was standing in a small room, the only light coming from a crack under the door.

"Ah, Isabelle," the man murmured into her ear. "You never cease to amaze."

She tried to wriggle out of his grasp, to make a sound loud enough to be heard in the hallway. It only seemed to please him. His right hand was still over her mouth, his left locked around her body, pinning her arms to her sides. Without loosening his grip, he leaned down and buried his face in the curve of her neck. Then he whispered in her ear.

"I knew you were extraordinary," he said. "Most people don't even have the courage to fight for their own lives. They go like sheep to the slaughter. But you . . ." He shifted his grip so he kept her mouth covered but freed the other hand to roam over the front of her body. The invasion spurred her to struggle again to get away, still to no avail.

"Don't be afraid, Isabelle. I'm not here to kill you." His breath was hot in her ear. "Not tonight, anyway."

She stopped fighting, because she realized it was getting her nowhere; in fact, it seemed to be arousing him.

"Since my employer is on the run, it's highly unlikely she'll make the final payment once the job is completed. Therefore, the contract is on hold." He ran his hand down her side, over her hip. She forced herself to stay still. "That's another first for me, you know."

His hand came up across the front of her body again, this time resting at the base of her throat. It climbed higher, until his fingers were wrapped around the front of her neck. He squeezed, hard enough to make her afraid he'd been lying about not killing her then and there. But then he relaxed his grip.

"If I take my hand off your mouth, are you going to scream?"

She shook her head. He turned her around so she was facing him, in some weird incarnation of an embrace.

"I'm afraid your friend Collins is going to live," he said. "It seems just having you near me affects my aim."

She stared up at him, anger trumping fear. "Who the hell *are* you?"

He smiled. "Just an average American boy who watched too many violent movies."

"That's bullshit. You're a goddamn sociopath."

"Sticks and stones, Isabelle. Sticks and stones." He brushed her hair back from her face, then sighed. "I'll be doing some work abroad. It seems like a good time to get out of the country. I hope you understand."

She nodded. She wasn't sure what else to do. All she knew for sure was that she was trapped in a closet with a murderer who seemed to think they were in the final scene of *Casablanca*.

"But I'll be back," he said. "One way or another, we'll see each other again. Or at least . . . I'll see you."

He kissed her on the mouth, long and hard. Isabelle was too stunned to try to fight him off. By the time she realized what was happening, he was gone. She opened the door as fast as she could, looked left and right down the hallway, but he'd already disappeared.

. . .

Later, when Isabelle looked back on all the things that had happened to her that day, she had a hard time deciding what was the most shocking. The blond man's perverse advances? The realization that Becky Belden was a homicidal bitch?

Or was it the way that Mac Collins' family had treated her?

The Collinses had arrived not ten minutes after she'd been groped in the broom closet, when she was still half scared the man was going to come back to finish her off. They'd walked in en masse—mother, father, two brothers, their wives, even his grandmother—and started raising hell and demanding information. Isabelle would've recognized them even if they hadn't been trumpeting his name to the shell-shocked staff; his family looked just like him, with their Waspy clothes and their air of supreme confidence.

She'd shied away from them, in no mood to face their fury. But they'd recognized her—no great trick considering that the news stations had been broadcasting her picture ad nauseam. And just when she'd expected them to flay her with their Ivy League vocabulary, they'd wrapped their arms around her and thanked her for saving his life.

Isabelle and his family waited five hours for Mac to get out of surgery, his two brothers taking turns going out to Starbucks, coming back with cardboard carriers full of double espressos and skinny lattes and assorted pastries. The hospital coffee, she gathered, was not even worth mentioning.

Still, though they must be dropping fifty dollars on each Starbucks run, they didn't strike her as snobs. They seemed too outdoorsy and down-to-earth—and they didn't seem to mind that their son had been going out with a woman who worked in a diner on the weekends.

The reason they knew about her job at the Cosmo, it turned out, was that Mac had actually told them about her. That fact, even more than his family's kindness, floored her.

As she sat with them in the waiting room, she tried not to think about the way she'd mistreated him, both in thought and in deed. She'd actually believed that he'd been a murderer—had misjudged and mistrusted him and nearly gotten him killed. She had no doubt that when he woke up, *if* he woke up, he was going to tell her to go straight to hell. It was only her guilt—the knowledge that she deserved every curse he might want to aim at her—that made her stick around, when all she really wanted to do was go home and cry.

At ten o'clock, when Isabelle was trying to concentrate on a game of gin rummy that Mac's sisters-in-law had dragged her into, a surgeon came out and told them he was going to live. The Collins men clapped each other on the back, and although

Mac's mother shed a tear or two, she didn't look at all surprised; Isabelle got the feeling she'd never let herself contemplate the possibility that he wouldn't pull through.

Although Mac was stable, the family wasn't going to be allowed to visit him until the next morning. His parents thanked the doctor profusely, asked for his card so they could send him a case of Scotch, and gathered the troops for a late dinner at their favorite Chinese restaurant. Isabelle begged off, and although his mother protested, his father pointed out that she looked like she was going to keel over. So the Collinses put her in a taxi, waving off her protests that it wasn't too late to take the subway. When she got to her apartment, she found they'd already paid the fare.

chapter 40

"I'll have two fried eggs, once over lightly. And I mean *lightly*. I don't like it when the yolk is all hard. Wheat toast, no butter. I mean, I want butter, but I want it on the *side*. Grapefruit juice, home fries, and a double order of bacon. Oh, and decaf coffee. And it better be decaf, because caffeine makes me jittery. You got that?"

"Yep."

"Are you sure? Don't you need to write it down?"

"I remember it."

"Then say it back to me."

Isabelle reeled off the man's order. When she got it right, he seemed somewhat disappointed. But she smiled at him, because bigger smiles meant bigger tips. She'd looked it up at the library and found out that a university had actually done research on it. Introduce yourself by name, put a smiley face on the check—according to the academics, it inspired the customer to open up his wallet. From what she'd seen so far, it actually worked.

Isabelle had been working at the Cosmo full-time for the past month, Becky Belden's disappearance having coincided with a regular waitress's departure for points west. Mr. and Mrs. Mendes had offered her the job, and Isabelle had jumped at it; she needed the money, and she was in no hurry to return to corporate America. The waitressing job might be hard on her feet, she reflected daily, but at least no one at the diner had tried to kill her yet.

"You take care of table six?" Mrs. Mendes asked, tapping a bright red fingernail on the countertop. "He ask for you special."

"I already put in the order. I just need to grab him some decaf."

"Good girl. Now go over to twenty-two. He ask for you special, too."

Isabelle pushed her hair back from where it was stuck on her sweaty forehead. "Mrs. M, you gotta stop trying to play matchmaker. Please?"

"But, kookla, you look so *depressed*."

"I—"

"Don't worry, honey. Soon you'll find a real job again, pretty college girl like you. And then a *husband* . . ."

"I'm not in the market for a husband, thanks very much."

"What about that handsome guy used to come in here?"

"You mean the one who got shot because of me?"

Mrs. Mendes nodded, her helmet of dyed-black hair not moving a millimeter. "Mmm, that one. Why he not come by for breakfast?"

"Because he got *shot* because of me, that's why."

"He's nice guy," Mrs. Mendes said with a shrug. "He don't hold a grudge."

"I wouldn't be so sure of that."

"What you don't know about men is a lot."

"Huh?"

"Table twenty-two," she said with a Mona Lisa smile, and disappeared into the kitchen.

In the twelve steps it took to get to the table, Isabelle tried to calculate the odds that Mrs. Mendes was putting her on. She also tried to wipe the sweat off her face, just in case the older woman was telling the truth.

She approached her customer from behind. He was wearing a baseball cap, so she couldn't tell who it was until she was standing beside him.

Mac Collins was ten pounds lighter, and his color didn't look quite right. Still, the sight of him—alive and well enough to walk into a diner late on a Thursday morning—made tears spring out of her eyes and run down her cheeks.

"Jesus," he said. "I was hoping you'd be glad to see me."

"Why the . . . What the . . . I am."

"You've got a funny way of showing it. Here, have a napkin. Sit down."

She blew her nose. "I have to . . ." She looked over at Mrs. Mendes, who was already pouring decaf at table six. She sat down and grabbed the other napkin.

"Are you okay?"

"Am *I* okay? What the hell difference does it make if *I'm* okay? I'm not the one who got shot."

"I realize that," he said. Then, a beat later: "*Are* you okay?"

"No," she said.

"What's wrong?"

"For chrissake, I almost got you killed. What do you *think* is wrong?"

"Oh." He seemed to consider it for a minute. "Is that why you didn't visit me in the hospital?"

She looked down at the paper place mat. "I sent you a get-well card."

"Actually," he said, "you sent me seven."

"I really wanted you to get well."

"I'm well. Reasonably well, anyway. Doctors say I won't be a hundred percent for a while. Could be a year before I can do everything I used to."

"That's awful."

"It's better than never."

Isabelle was digesting this when Mrs. Mendes came to the table. "So what I can get you?" she asked. "Is a little early for tuna melt, I think. You want pancake maybe?"

Mac ordered an omelet. Isabelle, whose stomach was in a variety of knots, just asked for coffee. Mrs. Mendes nodded at Mac, winked at Isabelle, and said she was brewing a fresh pot.

Isabelle sat across from him, nervous fingers fiddling with her necklace, utterly clueless about what to say. How could she even begin to apologize to him?

"That's pretty," he said.

"Huh?"

"The necklace. Is it new?"

She looked down at the gold chain, which held a pendant in the shape of the letter "I." "My sister sent it to me for my birthday," she said. "Came from Tiffany's. In the blue box and everything."

Mac shifted in his seat, trying to find a comfortable position in the vinyl booth. "I forgot you had a sister."

"She's a plastic surgeon in L.A. We never had a whole lot in common. But after everything that happened—you know, when it all hit the news, I think she kind of felt guilty. We've been talking a lot, anyway."

"That's good. Isn't it?"

"Yeah, I guess. She and her husband may come visit with the twins at Christmas, do all the tourist stuff. Radio City and all that."

"Sounds like it's right up your alley."

Her lips formed the hint of a smile. "Yeah, it is."

"So when was your birthday?"

"Last week. Twenty-five."

"A milestone."

Mrs. Mendes came back, with the coffeepot in one hand and two large Lucite picture frames under her arm. She filled the cups and put the pot on the table, then brandished one of the frames, which contained the *Daily News* front page from the day after Mac had been shot. The headline said, OFF THE AIR, in huge type; in a smaller font, the subhead read, MANNERS MAVEN BECKY BELDEN FLEES SOUNDSTAGE AFTER MURDER PLOT REVEALED!

Mrs. Mendes proffered the paper, along with a black Sharpie. "You autograph, okay?"

Mac looked at it, then shook his head. "Um . . . I don't think so."

"No? How come?" She cast a disapproving look at Isabelle. "You just like this girl. She won't sign, neither."

Mac looked more amused than mad. "Smart lady," he said.

"How about this one?"

She displayed the second frame, this one containing the *Post.* It was from the same day; the headline said, ISABELLE GIVES 'EM HELL! The subhead read, JILTED BRIDE SAVES EXEC, BESTS BECKY IN MURDER PLOT SHOWDOWN! Mac shook his head.

"No?" Mrs. Mendes shrugged. "Too bad. I figure I give it a try, no? Anyway, I be back with your food. Breakfast for you on the house."

She slunk back to the kitchen on her stiletto heels. Isabelle watched her go, feeling mortified.

"Sorry about that," she said.

"She's nuts, isn't she?"

"A little. I had to talk her out of putting those up in the window with a big picture of me. She thought it'd be good for business."

He nodded. After a minute, he took a sip of his coffee and said, "I'm not mad at you, you know."

"You're not?"

"No."

"But . . . you have to be. You'd have to be a crazy person not to hate my guts."

"Well, then, maybe I'm as nutsy as your boss."

"Mac, you almost died. And it was all my fault."

"No, it wasn't."

"Yes, it—"

"Just shut up, okay? I know everything that happened. The cops practically pitched a tent in my hospital room, and apparently, Friedrich and Bing have been singing at the top of their lungs. I know how everything went down before I got shot and after, and . . ." He coughed, took a sip of coffee, waited to catch his breath. "And I understand why you believed what you believed. It's hardly your fault, considering those bastards tried to frame me."

Isabelle's cup was halfway to her mouth. She put it down with a shaky hand, sloshing coffee on the tabletop. "They did?"

"No one told you?" Isabelle shook her head. "It was those counterfeit e-mails Chesbro found. The ones that made him go on the run."

"I was wondering about those. But I guess I figured since Kenny was so freaked out, he just got confused about who they were from."

"Hardly. Bing stockpiled them in case everything went to hell. Bastard was a computer science major as an undergrad. He made the e-mails look like they'd come from me, and I was behind the whole scheme. Recipients were a bunch of untraceable Hotmail and Yahoo! accounts. He'd also concocted a whole paper trail—letters, memos, phony contracts. If things went south, he was going to plant them and let me take the fall."

"But why you?"

Mac shrugged. "There weren't too many of us at the top at BBM, just the three of them and me and maybe a handful of other people, so they didn't have a lot of choice. But apparently, the major reason was, they thought that out of everyone on the senior staff, I was the biggest threat. I was working my ass off trying to figure out what was wrong with our numbers, and running the in-house consulting group gave me access to every other department. If there's anyone who could've connected the dots, it was me."

"So why didn't they just, you know . . ."

"Kill me?" His mouth twisted into a smirk. "As long as I was doing my job and not asking the wrong questions, Becky considered me an asset. But the minute they thought I was onto them, they would've gotten rid of me. And if the truth about the insurance scam ever came out, they were going to pin it all on me. Dead or alive."

"That's crazy."

"Yeah. But Becky Belden didn't get to the top by playing it safe."

"I guess." She rubbed the back of her head, which was starting to ache. "Are you sick of talking about all this?"

"Definitely. But if there's something you need to know, ask me and let's get it over with."

"There's something that doesn't make sense to me. Why would Becky give Kenny so much publicity if she wanted him to disappear?"

"Unfortunately, I know the answer to that."

"Which is?"

"She figured that by getting the word out, there was no place he could hide. When someone spotted him and called the tip line, they were going to get rid of him and make it look like he killed himself. Meanwhile Becky had her people sitting on his family, pretending to take care of them." He shook his head. "What an evil bitch."

"But Kenny—" Isabelle's voice clogged in her throat. "If it weren't for me, he never would've been found. I led them right to him. And then I got you—"

"Isabelle, stop it. The way I look at it, you saved my ass. End of conversation."

"But I was so unfair to you. I decided you were guilty, and I never even gave you a chance to explain. That night in the store-room—"

"The what?"

She explained it to him, how she'd thought she recognized his shoes and his voice and his turns of phrase. Despite his assurances, she was afraid he'd be angry, but he just laughed.

"Christ, Isabelle, that's classic MBA-speak. 'Pushing back,' 'going forward,' 'executing on the idea.' We all talk like that."

"You do?"

"Yeah. And we all pretty much dress alike, too. Don't beat yourself up about it. And as for what Kenny told you . . . for chrissake, of *course*, you thought I was guilty. That's what they intended all along."

Isabelle shook her head. "It was pretty much the perfect crime, wasn't it? If it hadn't been for that freakish thing with Kenny, they could've gone on forever, just killing people and pocketing the cash."

"Actually," he said, "that's where you're wrong."

chapter 41

"i don't understand," Isabelle said. It felt like she was saying that a lot lately.

Mac tapped his fingers on the tabletop. "Do you remember a couple months ago, some Japanese publishers came for a site visit?"

Isabelle thought about it. "Yeah, I do. It was right after I started working for Lisa. Bing was mad at me because she blew them off."

"Well, Bing would've been a hell of a lot madder if he'd known why they were really there." She saw the hint of a smile tug at the corner of his mouth. "When you and I and Becky were in the dressing room, I told you she used different insurance companies all over the world so no one would get suspicious. Well, apparently, someone did."

"You mean—"

"Those guys weren't publishers. They were insurance investigators from Tokyo. Apparently, Friedrich had set up policies with two of their firm's sister companies in Asia, never thinking that they'd put two and two together."

"But they did? They knew what she was up to?"

"Not all of it. But they had a feeling something wasn't right, and there was potentially a lot of money at stake, so they sent the investigators to get a look at BBM from the inside. But they weren't moving too fast. A lot more—" He erupted into another coughing fit, longer this time. When it was over, he'd gone two shades whiter. "What I was trying to say is, a lot more people might've died before they figured out what she was up to."

"Are you okay? You're really pale. Maybe it's too soon for you to be—"

"Christ, I'm fine. It feels good to be somewhere other than flat on my back. I'm just a little weak still, that's all. Okay?"

She dabbed her eyes with the damp napkin. "Okay."

"Good. Is there anything else you want to know?"

"Just . . . what about Lisa? If she and Becky were such old friends, why would she have her killed, too?"

Mac swallowed some water, wincing like it hurt his throat. "According to Friedrich, Becky always thought she was a pain in the neck—she was constantly bugging her to do some hare-brained project or another. Plus, she fit the pattern for the insurance scheme. And since she was fairly high up in the organization and she'd been around forever, killing her made for a big payday. A couple million at least."

"Oh."

The ensuing silence made Isabelle feel awkward, like they were suddenly on a blind date. She poured sugar into her coffee, drank some, and realized she must've already sweetened it. It tasted like a glazed doughnut.

"Have you . . . If you've been talking to the cops a lot, do you know what happened to Becky? Does anybody know where she is?"

He shrugged, then grimaced, like it hurt his incision. "My guess is, she's comfortably ensconced in some island country with no extradition."

"Do you think they'll ever catch her?"

"I'd like to say yes, but frankly, I think she's too smart. Also too damn rich."

They drank their coffee in silence while Isabelle tried to work up the courage to ask him one more question. It took a while.

"Um, I was wondering something," she said finally. "Before . . . when I thought you were in on the whole plot, because of what Kenny said, I thought you'd been hanging around with me because, you know . . ." She took a nervous sip of coffee, sloshed some again on the tabletop. "Because you had to keep an eye on me." Feeling her bravado start to slip, she kept her eyes on the place mat. "And now that I know you weren't up to anything like that, I was wondering, well . . . why *did* you?"

He was silent for a long beat. Isabelle still didn't have the guts to look him in the eye.

"Are you asking me why I wanted to spend time with you?"

"I guess. Yeah."

"Did it ever occur to you that maybe I just enjoyed your company?" She opened her mouth to answer, but no sound came out. She heard him put down his cup, felt the table shift as he leaned back in the booth. "Okay, let me come clean here," he said. "Do you remember when we first met, when I came down to schedule a meeting with Lisa? And then I canceled it the next day?"

She ventured a peek. Then a nod.

"Well, the truth is, there *was* no meeting. The truth is, I saw you in the audience at the TV show, and I thought you were so damn cute I asked around until I found out who you were, all the while hoping like hell that you weren't some tourist from Arkansas. And then, like some idiotic kid, I went to your office and told a giant fib so I could meet you. Now, does *that* do a little something to combat your low self-esteem?"

Isabelle gulped. "Er . . . yes."

"The only problem was, since the company was a mess and I was working like a dog and I hadn't had an actual relationship in God knows when, I was in no position to do right by you. And for that, I apologize."

"It's okay," she said automatically. Then, after thinking it over some more, she said, "It's really okay. After what happened with Laurence, I didn't exactly have my head screwed on straight, either."

"And now?"

She cracked a small smile. "It's an ongoing project."

He smiled back. "Okay, well, given that, can I ask *you* something?" She nodded. "Do you think we could maybe act like two normal people who haven't been through some crazy thing and just see each other? Without a lot of melodrama?"

For a second, she was afraid she was misunderstanding him. "You, uh, want to date me?"

"That's the idea. Until I get my strength back enough to do something friendlier."

"Well . . . okay."

"Is that a yes?"

"That's a yes."

He reached across the table and squeezed her hand. "And one more thing."

"What's that?"

"I want you to let me express my appreciation for saving my life. And before you say anything, you should know that I have a particular method in mind."

"What's that?"

"I intend," he said, "to buy you some goddamn furniture."

.   .   .

Isabelle filled her mug with Earl Grey tea and padded across the living room to her new ergonomic chair—which, along with a fancy new modular desk from Pottery Barn, had come from Mac. He'd suggested a couch, which she knew made perfect sense, but she'd chosen the desk just the same.

She sat down and flipped through the thick pile of pages covered in her barely legible scrawl. She'd been making notes for the past two weeks, working nights when she came home from the diner, and she finally felt ready to start writing.

It'd felt strange, reliving all that had happened with an eye toward turning it into a novel—figuring out the beats of the story, when to stick to the truth and when to take artistic license. She remembered how fired up she'd been about using the BBM saga as her ticket out of poverty, and was vaguely embarrassed by it. The stakes seemed so much higher, the story so much more poignant; now all she wanted to do was tell it well. She wanted to do it justice.

Isabelle turned on the computer and stared at the empty file. She contemplated making herself some microwave popcorn, but she forced herself to concentrate. She'd turned down Mac's invitation to come over and watch a video, so she had no choice but to get to work; he was sure to ask her about her progress the next day. She'd promised herself she'd do at least five pages, then reward herself with a late-night episode of *Law & Order* and one of the Klondike bars in her freezer.

She sighed, then remembered something one of her college professors had told her. Just get something on the page so you have something to work with; you can always erase it later.

She turned back to the keyboard.

Annabelle Lincoln, she wrote, *had never been good at job interviews.*